NO
MAN'S
LAND

NO
MAN'S
LAND

William Fairchild

BANTAM BOOKS
TORONTO · NEW YORK · LONDON · SYDNEY · AUCKLAND

NO MAN'S LAND

*A Bantam Book / published by arrangement
with the author*

PRINTING HISTORY
Originally titled The Poppy Factory,
published in Great Britain 1987
Bantam edition / January 1989
All rights reserved.
Copyright © 1987 by William Fairchild Productions Ltd.
Book design by Maria Carella

Library of Congress Cataloging-in-Publication Data

Fairchild, William.
  No man's land.

  I. Title.
PR6011.A395N6 1989   823'.912   88-19409
ISBN 0-553-05331-0

PRINTED IN THE UNITED STATES OF AMERICA
DH   0 9 8 7 6 5 4 3 2 1

FOR IAN MAXWELL

My conscience hath a thousand several tongues,
And every tongue brings in a several tale,
And every tale condemns me for a villain.

William Shakespeare, *Richard III*

During four long years the sole internationalism . . . had been
that of deserters from all the warring nations. . . . Outlawed,
these men lived—at least they *lived* . . . under certain parts of
the front line . . . recognizing no rights and no rules save of their
own making. . . .

Osbert Sitwell,
Laughter in the Next Room

PART 1

THE
BIRTHDAY
PRESENT

CHAPTER 1

My beginnings were hardly auspicious. My father was killed in the battle for Caen in the late summer of 1944 just six months before my birth and I was plucked into the world by Caesarean operation because my mother's doctors considered her in too weak a state to survive a normal delivery. Their diagnosis was undoubtedly correct but their skills failed to save her. She never left the hospital and died there when I was six weeks old. I still dream of her but cannot see her face. I don't dream of my father. They are no more than a pair of photographs in a folding red leather frame, its edges fraying, old, but their eyes remain youthful and smiling, alive with confidence and hope, those of two strangers, dead now for more than thirty years.

My paternal grandfather, General Adrian Garrard, took immediate possession of my infant self on the grounds that he enjoyed far better financial resources than my mother's parents and, furthermore, that I bore his name. He was a formidable adversary if balked, and I doubt if plain Mr. and Mrs. Simms living in a semidetached in Rickmansworth put up much of an argument, but if they did, I am sure he would have clinched his victory by reminding them that their daughter had spent the last five years of her life under his roof, first as his secretary and finally as the wife of his son, my father.

I was installed in his large Cornish manor house under the immediate care of his housekeeper, Miss Hilda Wilkins. She had a purple birthmark on her left cheek, jet black hair, green eyes, and I decided early on that she was a witch. There seemed no reason to revise this opinion when I discovered later that before entering my grandfather's employ she had served during the war as a senior NCO in the Auxiliary Territorial Service and clearly hankered after her days of martial glory when she could put the fear of Old Nick into fledgling privates. Denied this pleasure, she did her best to put it into me instead, especially during what were designated recreation periods when she insisted on our playing cowboys and Indians together. She was always the cowboys while I represented some unfortunate redskin brave, often being tied to a tree with one of her long kitchen towels so that she could take potshots at me with a toy pistol whose explosive caps made a hideous noise, frightening the birds out of the garden and me out of my wits.

My grandfather gave me another sort of a gun for my seventh birthday, an old Colt revolver which, he had repeatedly informed me, was a relic of *his* war, the great one. He must have brought it into my room late on the previous night because when I woke, it was lying on the bedside table, naked of any festive paper, cold and ugly, its barrel pointing toward me. Before I could bring myself to touch it, Miss Wilkins came in with a box of assorted chocolates and oohed and aahed her delight.

"What a *privileged* boy you are, Adrian. That revolver is the general's most prized possession. Mind you never lose it."

I'd already decided to throw the thing into the lake at the bottom of the garden at the first possible opportunity, but assured her I'd take the very greatest care of it. She was followed by Fred Barnes, carrying an electric train set which I'd admired in a shop window the last time he'd taken me to the cinema in Truro. Fred, a faith healer and reputed to be able to work miracles, was the absolute antithesis of Miss Wilkins. I kept asking him to wave his magic wand and make her disappear, but he simply smiled and assured me there was good in everyone if you only knew where to look for it. He lived in a cottage two miles away and was the only one of my grandfather's friends I liked. The rest seemed to spend their lives hunting foxes or shooting birds. I couldn't imagine Fred killing anything. Miss Wilkins disapproved of him for two principal reasons. He practiced "mumbo jumbo" and he was not "county."

"He met the general in the First War," she would say darkly, "and we all know no good ever came of *that*. Still, I suppose that's why he's always in and out of the house. You can never tell with *men*."

I tore the wrappings off Fred's present while he examined the revolver, expertly spinning the chamber, squinting through its holes.

"That's all right then," he said. "The bugger's not loaded."

"Of course not, Mr. Barnes," Miss Wilkins said reprovingly. "Generals aren't barmy."

"I've known a few that were," said Fred and winked at me as we began to assemble the railway lines.

That afternoon my grandfather summoned me to join him for a stroll in the garden.

"Bring the Colt, boy. Get used to handling it."

I fetched the thing from the room, first putting on a pair of woolen gloves, a kind of insulation.

Far from strolling, he never even walked in a normal fashion but always marched as though keeping time with some invisible military band. A pronounced limp did nothing to impede the rapidity of his progress but afforded it an alarming corkscrew motion, giving the impression to anyone accompanying him that he was constantly on the verge of making a sharp alteration of course. Such a stroll, like most activities shared with him, meant remaining constantly on the alert for the unexpected. There were only two things to do with a gammy leg, he used to say. First train it to behave properly, then forget it. Mind over matter, a question of discipline.

"A birthday's as good a time as any for a family powwow," he said as we set off, heads up, chests out, swinging those arms. "Mine was November the eleventh, eighteen ninety-five, Adrian. I suppose that sounds like the Middle Ages to you?"

It sounded like prehistory, but I kept silent and tried to look impressed.

"Day of peace, two minutes' silence, Cenotaph, etcetera. But of course they hadn't built it then."

He laughed. The sound was sudden and unexpected like the bark of an unseen dog.

"Nineteen years old when my war started. Twenty-three when I finished it. A lot never did. Hell of a lot."

I imagined hordes of soldiers, fed up with the whole noisy

business, throwing down their rifles and running away. Sensible chaps, I thought.

"Deserters?" I asked.

He came to a sudden halt, grabbed the cane which he carried tucked under his left arm and slashed at a passing butterfly.

"The dead," he said solemnly. "The ones who didn't come back." For a brief moment the tip of the cane rested against his right temple in mute salute, then we were on the move again.

"Over forty when the next lot began. Never got out of Whitehall. That was your father's war, Adrian."

I nodded, thinking it odd that each generation should lay titular claim to its particular conflict. I had no wish for one of my own.

"I'd have christened you George after him except for breaking the tradition. Adrian—George, Adrian—George, right down through the centuries. Don't mind being an Adrian like me, do you?"

Apart from the fact of our sharing it, I quite liked the name so I was able to shake my head with some semblance of enthusiasm.

"Proud of your father aren't you, boy? Proud of my son George?"

I'd spilt Ovaltine over the young face in the old frame the evening before and spent a good hour trying to remove it. Bits had oozed under the glass giving my father a discolored ear and a black eye. It had been quite a tricky job.

"Oh yes," I gasped, trying to keep up without breaking into a trot. The weight of the revolver in my hands didn't make it any easier.

"Fine soldier. Brave man. A splendid death."

His boots stamped into the gravel path as though it were a parade ground. He kept a photograph of the late Field Marshal Haig on the desk in his study, and I'd once surprised him holding it in one hand while he stroked his own moustache with the other.

"Do try and keep up, boy. Difficult to carry on a conversation if you break step."

He told me, not for the first time, how my father had died. "Tackled a German machine gun nest single-handed. Shot clean through the head by a damned sniper. But he'd put that gun out of action first and all its crew. Saved God knows how many of his own men's lives. Splendid."

I remembered the spilt Ovaltine and imagined my father's shattered face, the blood not oozing, but spurting.

"Got the D.S.O. for it. But you know all about that."

I certainly did. The cross lay next to his own on the red velvet bed of a glass-topped table in the dining room. He would pause for a moment in front of the pair of them before each meal, perhaps uttering a silent grace.

"They'll be yours when I'm gone. His D.S.O. and mine. Should have been the V.C."

I wasn't sure which he meant, his own or his son's, and didn't ask. To me medals seemed dead things, like so many of those who had won them. He came to an abrupt halt beside one of Miss Wilkins's execution trees.

"Your mother didn't want to keep his decoration. What do you think of that, eh?"

I didn't know what to think, but wished suddenly and violently that she was still alive. Never having known her, I had never cried for her, but now I felt unexpected tears pricking my eyes. I turned away and stared down the length of the garden and said the first thing that came into my head.

"Did she say that here?"

"Yes, as a matter of fact she did." He sounded surprised. "In this garden. A month after your father was killed."

I felt his hands on my shoulders, turning me round to face him. "Look, old boy," he said earnestly. "I tried my hardest to comfort her, make her get things into proportion, see them straight. He'd died to save his men, I told her, died bravely, with honor. She should feel proud. . . ."

He broke off, swished at the daisies with his cane.

"And then she hit me," he said quietly. "Struck me in the face."

I thought wildly of a comedy film about army recruits Fred Barnes had taken me to see. There had been scenes showing Defaulters' Parades.

"Accused-off-caps!" "What-is-this-man's-crime-Sarnt-Major?" "Struck-the-general-in-the-face-sah!"

"She accused me," my grandfather was saying. "Told me I was responsible for my son's death."

I saw Miss Wilkins coming out of the kitchen door wearing Wellington boots and her old battle-dress jacket.

"She was overwrought, of course," my grandfather said, "but

she meant it." He whacked at the tree, glared at the wounded wood as though daring it to bleed.

"She swore she'd never let you go into the army, Adrian." His voice suddenly seemed faint, distant, even farther away than Miss Wilkins.

"We've always been soldiers. All the men in the family. Your mother didn't understand that. Didn't want to."

"Mons!" yelled Miss Wilkins. "Vimy! Heel!"

"She's dead," I said, but he was staring at the approaching dogs and I don't think he heard.

"She wasn't one of us," he said. "More's the pity."

I suppose I had always hated him but until that moment had never allowed myself to admit it.

"She was my mother," I shouted. "I love her. It was my fault she died." Then I ran at him, lunging out with both fists. He swung the cane upward, its tip resting against my chest, easily holding me away from him. But he looked afraid.

"Steady, old chap. Can't blame yourself for that. Some women are strong. Others—well, not strong enough."

I remember stepping back, raising the revolver, pointing it between his eyes.

"I wish it *was* loaded," I screamed and pulled the trigger.

For a dreadful moment I thought Fred Barnes had made a mistake, that I really had shot him.

The blood drained from his face, and chalk white, he swayed sideways, leaning against the tree for support. He was mumbling something, but I could not distinguish the words. I was aware of a soft thud as the revolver fell from my hand to the grass. Then slowly he pushed himself upright, came toward me and very gently put both arms around me, holding me close against him.

"That's right, my boy," he said, and I'd never known his voice to sound like that before, so quiet that it was little more than a whisper, so full of pain that it might have been a prayer for forgiveness.

"That's right—when you decide to shoot, don't hesitate. Don't ever do that."

Miss Wilkins spoke from close beside us, a strident shriek. "God almighty, general! What's up? You're crying."

I felt his arms relax and wriggled free. I couldn't look at him.

"Angry," I heard him mutter. "Bloody angry."

"What's the boy done now?" demanded Miss Wilkins and tried to grab me.

"Not with him, woman. With myself." His voice rose to a shout. "And I'm not the kind who weeps, for Christ's sake!"

But as I ran away from them with Mons and Vimy leaping up on either side, I felt moisture on my forehead and, wiping it away, tasted on my palm the salt of his tears.

CHAPTER 2

Fred Barnes caught up with me later that same evening on the main road where I was trying to hitch a lift to Truro. Trapped like a mesmerized rabbit in the headlight beams of my grandfather's Bentley, I surrendered without a struggle once he had assured me he was alone. There wasn't much alternative. I had neither money nor plans and was beginning to feel uncomfortably hungry.

"Best come home," he said.

"It's not my home. It never was my home."

"Don't you worry about the general. Him and me had a talk. He won't bite your head off."

"I'm not staying," I said.

"We'll see about that. Leave it all to me. Fancy one of Miss Wilkins's fish pies for supper?"

It was warm in the car and the cowboy sharpshooter, for all her shortcomings, was in the cordon bleu class when it came to pies. Nevertheless I wasn't lulled into any false sense of security.

"Did you ever meet my mother, Fred?"

His hands tightened on the wheel as we turned into the drive.

"Of course I did."

"What was she like?"

"She was like Katherine."

"Katherine?"

"Your grandmother. No blood relation but the same sort."

"Strong?"

Gravel crunched beneath the wheels as he braked in front of the house and turned to look at me.

"Strong and faithful, young Adrian. Lovely, too. Just like Katherine."

I held tightly to Fred's hand as we went into the house in case we should see my grandfather, but there was no sign of him.

The fish pie was excellent and so was the extra-strength Ovaltine which Fred brought with it, but I couldn't sleep. After a while I turned on the light and picked up the red-framed photograph. If I stared at my mother's face for long enough, I hoped I might drop off and see it for the first time in my dreams. The idea didn't work. I was still awake an hour later when I heard my grandfather's heavy tread on the stairs. In a panic I switched off the light, but either he hadn't noticed or had chosen to ignore it. I heard the door of his room slam shut and began desperately counting sheep. That didn't work either and eventually I knew I'd have to go to the lavatory or risk wetting the bed. Wet beds were regarded by my grandfather as betraying a lack of discipline so I crept past his door and went to the bathroom. On the way back I saw a thin shaft of light slanting across the passage from his room. I'd decided to risk running past it rather than spend the rest of the night in the passage when I heard Fred's voice behind the half-opened door.

"You may have thought we'd finished the argument downstairs. I didn't. And I wouldn't drink any more if I were you."

"Bugger off, Fred, for God's sake. Leave me alone."

"I've phoned his other grandparents. Made all the arrangements. They're anxious to help. Take my advice. Let him go for both your sakes."

There was a long pause. I heard the clink of a glass being set down on the marble-topped bedside table.

"I let a man go once, Fred."

"That's got nothing to do with it."

"It has everything to do with it."

"All right," Fred Barnes said, "and it damned nearly ruined your life with Katherine. You listened to me then. Listen now."

"You're not suggesting I tell him, too, are you?"

"'Course not. He's only a kid."

"I told you what he did with that gun. He wanted to kill me."

I heard the harsh dog-laugh and pressed myself back against the wall.

"He pulled the trigger. Actually pulled it. More than I could do when it mattered. But I couldn't know then. I couldn't, could I, Fred?"

I realized with a sense of shock that the slurred quavering words were not simply due to drink but to the imminence of tears.

"You couldn't," Fred said. "We all know that. But you've clung on to your damn stupid unreasonable guilt, and it's built up inside you like a poison. Don't let it infect him too. That's all I'm saying."

"Pass me that brandy, Fred."

"If I were you . . ."

"You're not me, for Christ's sake!"

"Let him go. For a time anyway. Till he's older. You can still keep in touch. All right?"

In the silence while my fate was being decided, I could visualize Fred Barnes pouring him another glass. For my own sake I hoped it was a small one. If my grandfather drank much more, he might decide to crash into my room and murder me. When he spoke again, his voice was so low that I could only just hear it.

"I wanted so much for that boy, Fred. I wanted him to realize all the dreams Katherine and I had. All the dreams his father had. All the dreams . . ."

"And his mother's," Fred said. "Well, perhaps he will. In his own way. I'll be back first thing in the morning. Good-night now."

He came out of the room, closed the door quietly behind him, turned toward the stairs without seeing me. I watched him as he went down to the hall, crossed it, and left the house. It took a long time because he moved very slowly as though almost exhausted.

When he was at last out of sight, I started to tiptoe toward my own room, but before I'd taken two steps, my grandfather's door flew open and he stood there in front of me barring my path. He was wearing his favorite dressing gown, the one in the colors of his old regiment, and his eyes were puffed and red, his cheeks flushed. We faced each other for what seemed like minutes, two enemies waiting for the other to make the first move. I tried to stand my ground but knew that my whole body was shaking.

Then, suddenly, he laughed. Not the dog-bark but rather a sort of muted yelp, weary, uncertain, full of unexpected sadness.

"Been to the latrines have you, my boy? That's a good fellow. Well done."

He leaned toward me, swaying a little. I braced myself for the blow. But instead he kissed me on the forehead with his wet, brandy-smelling lips.

"Just like a good soldier," he said as he skirted past me. "Just like I'd always hoped."

They were the last words I ever heard him speak.

He did not appear for breakfast next day and I ate with Fred Barnes and Miss Wilkins in the kitchen. She kept banging cups and plates on the scrubbed wooden table in a disapproving manner while he explained carefully and firmly that he would drive me to my mother's parents' home in Rickmansworth that morning for what he described as "a trial period."

"The general has spoken to them on the telephone, Adrian. They look forward to welcoming you. All concerned are agreed it's for the best." Miss Wilkins rammed burnt toast into the rack and snorted.

"All," he repeated firmly.

I hadn't been consulted but that didn't worry me. My vote would simply have endorsed the majority decision.

Fred helped me pack my two suitcases, carefully wrapping the twin red-framed photographs in tissue paper.

"They'll be pleased to see those," he said.

"Shouldn't I say good-bye to my grandfather?"

"Best not just now. He's busy attending to his correspondence. Got a big shoot to organize for next week. You could write to him when you're settled in, though, keep in touch. He'd like that."

Halfway down the drive I turned to look back at the house. My grandfather was standing outside the front door, the cane raised in his right hand, touching his cap. It might have been a gesture of farewell or simply an ironic salute to the riddance of bad rubbish. At the gates we nearly ran over one of the Labradors. Miss Wilkins burst through the rhododendron bushes.

"Vimy!" she shrieked. "Mons! Heel!"

She didn't look at the car.

"Bloody dogs," Fred Barnes muttered and swung out into the road.

I slept most of the way to Rickmansworth, and we'd reached its outskirts before I remembered the revolver. I hated the thing, but it had been a birthday present, and I felt a tinge of guilt in abandoning it.

"Safer with the general," Fred said gruffly. "Scare the daylights out of this place. Peaceful lot by the look of them."

I stared at the tidy rows of neat little houses and remembered something else.

"What were you two arguing about last night?"

"You should have been in bed and asleep, young Adrian."

"I had to pee."

"Nothing of any consequence," Fred said. "Just discussing our old war. You'll be happy here in your new home."

"How do you know?"

"I'm psychic," Fred said and laughed.

"Grandpa had been drinking, hadn't he?"

"We'd both had a bit."

"He sounded miserable. As if he was going to cry."

"Rubbish."

"Miss Wilkins said he was crying yesterday. You know, in the garden, when I . . ."

"Woman's imagination," Fred said scornfully. "The general *crying*? You know him better than to believe a thing like that, young Adrian."

It was to be many years before I knew him well enough.

My maternal grandfather owned a small bookshop and his wife was active in local politics. She believed fervently in the future according to Mr. Attlee, while he cherished the past as exemplified by "good old Winston."

Politically divided, they were in other respects united, including, I suppose, after their fashion, that of love.

Ten minutes after Fred Barnes had left, they asked me to call them by their first names, which were Richard and Naomi.

"No ranks here," Naomi said briskly. "Everyone equal. I'm sure it'll make a nice change after what you've been used to, Adrian."

I tried to show them the photograph of my mother, their only child, but they closed their nonexistent ranks in assumed indifference.

"We've put all that behind us," Richard said. "What's over is over."

His normally bright eyes were momentarily dulled with pain. It didn't seem over for him.

"If we'd had the National Health Service then," Naomi said, "Christine would be alive today."

Christine. I must have been aware of her name, but I'd forgotten it and felt ashamed. To make amends I spoke it aloud each evening when I said good-night to the twin photographs. I didn't address my father as George. That would have been going too far, lèse majesté.

The house had three bedrooms and at first I believed that mine, the smallest, had once belonged to my mother. I was wrong.

"We moved here from London after the war," Naomi said. "Richard was attached to the Ministry of Transport in those days. Reserved occupation."

"I was an Air Raid Warden as well," Richard added quickly, in case I was getting any false ideas. "Naomi drove an ambulance."

"That was after Russia came in," his wife said, keeping the record straight.

When I'd been in residence a week, Richard took me in his Hillman Minx to see the bookshop. It didn't appear to have many customers.

"Trade's quiet," he said, wistfully eyeing the crowded shelves. "Makes you feel sorry for all those writers."

He took a feather duster from a drawer, flicked it expertly across the top of a row of books.

"Christine always wanted to be one, you know," he said. "Her English reports from school were most encouraging. I paid for her to have a typing course afterward. That's how she came to get the job with your other grandfather. She helped him with his books."

"He wrote *books*?"

The idea of the general as any kind of author flabbergasted me.

"Only technical stuff," Richard said dismissively. "The deployment of tanks in battle, advantages of the mobile attack column, that sort of thing."

"Did my mother type them for him?"

Richard winked knowingly. "A bit more than that, if you ask me. Put them into some sort of English, I shouldn't wonder."

He grinned suddenly.

"Life's funny, isn't it? If she hadn't gone there, she wouldn't have met your father . . ."

He dropped the duster into its drawer, banged it shut.

"If you ever think of trying to be an author, Adrian, you just remember those shelves. It's sad having to brush dust off a book before anyone's even read it."

If there can ever be a particular moment for making such a decision, I think it was then that I decided to be a writer. I made it because it would be something which at last I could share with my mother, something which would draw us closer. I wanted to know more of her. I wanted to know everything.

"Did you keep anything she wrote?" I asked.

Richard shook his head and quickly changed the subject. It was only the second time he or Naomi had mentioned my mother's name and it was also the last. What's over is over.

"The general has been very generous in the matter of your allowance," he said. "No problems about education and so forth."

This, I felt, was the true reason for our visit to the shop. He didn't care to risk mentioning such financial nepotism in front of Naomi nor for that matter anything complimentary about my other grandfather. At the same time I realized that Fred's "trial period" had been no more than a euphemism. For better or worse I'd been sentenced without the option to a lengthy term in Rickmansworth.

"A generous general," Richard said, enjoying the alliteration.

Apart from school and university, I lived with them for the next sixteen years, before moving by mutual agreement to a small basement flat in London. Richard called it spreading my wings, and Naomi hoped I would add a Socialist vote in the Chelsea borough elections, where, she said, it was much needed. She died four years later in the spring of 1972, and driving down for the funeral, I experienced some difficulty in recognizing the right house. In that street each looked exactly like its neighbor, private but anonymous. Richard followed her a few months later. They were two of the nicest people I've ever known, yet when both had gone, I realized I had never really known them at all. Perhaps, like the house, they were built that way.

The general lived on, now in his seventy-eighth year. Mindful of Fred Barnes's admonition to keep in touch, I had sent him a series of brief ritual postcards when on holiday or on a school trip abroad, perhaps subconsciously comforted by the thought that the Channel between us would prevent him rushing out to kidnap me. I had never written to him while in England but this seemed an appropriate moment to do so. The cards had required no opening form of address, and I debated with myself for some time as to which to use. Dear General seemed too impersonal. Dear Grandfather too pompous. I settled for the diminutive of childhood.

September 12th, 1972

Dear Grandpa,

You may have heard the sad news that both Richard and Naomi have died. They were always so good to me and I shall miss them dreadfully. I know they could not have afforded to give me the sort of education I have enjoyed as a result of your generosity. I've never really thanked you properly for this, and I should like to do so now from the bottom of my heart.

I hope you won't think it's been wasted. I know you have been the author of several books on military subjects and that my mother always wanted to become a writer herself. Well, you may remember my sending you a card from Italy saying that I'd decided to try my hand at it too. Since then, I've managed to finish a novel and have recently signed a contract to work on a new film. They pay well and with luck it may lead to others.

I do hope you are keeping fit. Please give my love to Fred Barnes . . .

I balked at offering my love to him and did not say that the novel, though finished, was as yet unpublished and, judging from the number of rejection slips it had already accumulated, most probably never would be. Nor did I mention that while the film might be considered new, its script, having previously passed through the experienced, if conflicting hands of at least three American experts in the art, most definitely wasn't. My present task, as expressly stated in the contract, was "to anglicize the dialogue where necessary and as agreed without altering its sense." This mammoth literary endeavor would be completed within three weeks and I would receive for it the sum of seven hundred and fifty pounds. My grandfather, I imagined, would find such details even more depressing and confusing than I did myself.

There had been no reply to any of the postcards and I didn't

expect one to this more formal communication. But it arrived a
week later, first class.

September 16th, 1972

Dear Adrian,

Your grandfather has asked me to thank you for your
letter of the 12th. He would have written himself but he's
had to go into hospital for a couple of weeks. Nothing
serious, just a bit of trouble with the old waterworks. I
tried faith healing first but the bladder does not, I fear,
respond to the laying on of hands. He's delighted to hear
about the film and wishes you all the best for it. So do I. If
it ever comes to Truro, I shall go and shout, "Author."
Everything at the house is much the same.

Miss Wilkins is still her usual happy self, thoroughly
enjoying every bit of bad news that's going. There's a new
pair of Ladradors, which she insists on calling Mons and
Vimy like their predecessors because she can't be
bothered to learn new names.

Don't worry about the general. Old soldiers never
die—they just get prostate trouble. He's really very fond
of you, you know, so try to keep in touch even when
you're in Hollywood.

All the best from your old friend,
Fred

The reference to Hollywood puzzled me until my agent told me
that the chief of the production company was sufficiently impressed
with my efforts at anglicizing his dialogue to wish me to go there for
the purpose of colloquializing the English translation of a Yugoslav
play about Tito and the partisans which he intended turning into a
movie. Then I remembered that Fred was psychic even if he
couldn't cure prostates. I rang him for further advice.

"Go," he said. "One cannot live by bread alone, but there's no
harm in earning a bit."

My agent said much the same. "It may not be art but it's
money. Simply say everything's great and go where the action is."

CHAPTER 3

The action was there all right but by the time I arrived its nature had changed along with the sex and identity of the production chief. This was now someone described by Spencer, her story editor, as Boss Lady. Spencer had been turning out screenplays since the thirties and the wounds showed. Starting a picture, he explained, was like starting a war and writers were the first casualties. He also warned me that Boss Lady didn't frig around and sure had balls. When I got to know her better, I found this to be physically inaccurate, but lacking the actuality, she compensated by continual use of the word. Tito and the partisans were balls. Spencer talked balls but had an unbreakable contract. She wanted to make important films about important subjects, not balls. The theory that art and commercial profit didn't mix was more balls. She was obsessed by the idea of an epic production based on what she called the hinges of history, more specifically those actions or moments of decision which had principally contributed to the fall of the Roman empire, the dismemberment of the British one and the emergence of the U.S.A. world-stage center. A trilogy in fact with the same stars appearing in different roles in each of the three acts and culminating in a challenging question mark: *Whither America?* That wasn't balls. That would give everyone something to think about.

It certainly did. As part of my early indoctrination procedure, I attended with Spencer the conference at which Boss Lady first

announced her plans. The others present did their best to reflect
her enthusiasm but clearly found it heavy going. Spencer looked
like a man about to go over the top once too often. I tried to look
eager. Boss Lady glanced down at her notepad to check the name,
then glared at me.

"You're British," she said. "What do you think, Mr. Garrard?"

"I think it's just great," I said.

She smiled at me and glared at Spencer. Spencer sighed.

That evening she invited me to a dinner party at her home in Bel
Air. Before I'd had too much to drink, she asked for my views
regarding the decline of Britain. I gave them, based largely, I must
confess, on a personal assessment of my grandfather's character.
Later, brandy added to wine, I contributed, courtesy of the late
Naomi, a few words on the fall of Rome. Too much power, I said, in
too few hands, the wrong ones.

We watched a rival's film in her private viewing theater and
drank more brandy.

"Balls," said Boss Lady when it ended, and everyone immediately agreed. Then they all went home.

"Watch it, kid," Spencer whispered as he left. "She may
appear beautifully constructed, but so's an A-bomb till it explodes."

My hostess opened a fresh bottle of Remy Martin.

"How about America?" she asked.

Just in time I remembered one of Richard's favorite quotations
from good old Winston.

"The torch has been passed to you," I said gravely. "It will burn
safe and bright in your keeping."

She brought two glasses over to the sofa, sat down next to me.

"How would you feel about writing the project?" she said.

I looked into her eyes. They did appear to be beautifully
constructed.

"Just great," I said.

"That's fine," she said. "I would too. You'll work with Spencer.
What's your first name?"

I told her.

"You got anywhere particular in mind to go right now, Adrian?"

I muttered something about my hotel.

"My bedroom's more comfortable," she said and smiled.

Over the next two and a half years *Whither America?* became in grinding succession *Why?*, *Distant Drums*, and finally *The Question*. Spencer dropped dead in a Santa Monica bar in the middle of *Drums*, and after delivering the eulogy at his funeral, Boss Lady informed me that her psychiatrist had recommended an unspecified period of celibacy. I knew all about her new lover, a well-heeled Texan, and wished her luck.

"Balls," she said and giggled through her mourning veil.

Personally and professionally on my own, I staggered through the rest of *Drums* and lurched wearily into *The Question*. This was completed during another palace revolution which resulted in the dethronement of Boss Lady. The new regime, after brief consideration, proclaimed that *Whither America?* had been crap at birth, growing crappier with each reincarnation. I didn't argue. Before leaving for England I received a letter from Venezuela. It was headed From the Desk of the Vice-President, and Boss Lady stated among other things that whereas the oil business presented her with a real challenge, all that movie stuff was just a load of balls.

My years in Hollywood had been both enjoyable and instructive, though not principally in the field of screenwriting. They had also delayed my reading the only written communication my grandfather ever sent me during his lifetime. It was waiting at the Chelsea flat, a white card printed with his address but lacking either prefix or signature and dated fourteen months previously. The porter had agreed to forward letters but I'd told him not to bother about postcards.

I have something I wish to discuss with you. Kindly arrange to call here as soon as possible.

I had received more elegant and pressing invitations so I allowed two days and the jet lag to pass before telephoning the house. Miss Wilkins answered, her tone a mixture of grief and disapproval, the latter predominating.

"The general passed away last month," she said.

I began stumblingly to tell her how sorry I was, but she cut me short.

"He's left me the house for my lifetime. After that it's yours."

"He wrote to me," I said, "but the card was not forwarded. Otherwise I'd—"

"He sent that the day after Mr. Barnes died. Almost a year and a half ago."

I felt stunned, couldn't accept it. Fred had seemed an integral everlasting part of my life, indestructible.

"Why didn't he tell me that?"

"Since you never got the card, it wouldn't have made any difference if he had, would it," Miss Wilkins said. Her voice had regained its customary asperity. There was even a trace of enjoyment in it. So much bad news crammed into one telephone conversation.

"Where've you been all this time anyway?"

"Hollywood," I said guiltily, "California."

She repeated the names, making them sound like Sodom and Gomorrah.

"The general's left a sealed packet for you," she said. "I'm to hand it to you personally."

I had never liked the house, but at least there had been life of a sort in it, particularly when Fred was there. Now, after nearly twenty-five years, there seemed to be only death, and Hilda Wilkins shared its brooding presence while waiting for it to claim her.

"The general was over eighty when he died," she said. "I doubt I'll ever see eighty."

Even the dogs were dead, the latest Mons and Vimy replacements buried beside their predecessors in the garden. She showed me their graves before we visited my grandfather's. I stared at the inscription on his headstone and tried, without success, to say a prayer.

I asked her where Fred Barnes was buried.

"Over there," she said. "The other side of the churchyard."

She might just as well have said on the other side of the tracks, the one reserved for those who were not "county."

"The general insisted on paying for his funeral," she said. "The headstone and everything."

I wanted to see it, but Miss Wilkins vetoed the idea. It was getting dark, and she must give me my grandfather's package before she went to bed.

"It's in his study. I'll hand it to you myself because that's what I promised him. There's cold meat and salad in the larder and your old room's ready if you want to stay till tomorrow."

The package was large and heavy, bound with thick string, the knots covered in blobs of red sealing wax. I guessed at least a part of its contents as soon as I took it from her.

"I'll say good-night then," Miss Wilkins said. "Nothing for me to stay up for."

It was a few minutes before half past six.

The Colt revolver lay on top of a buff-colored envelope. Beneath that was another bulky parcel wrapped in grey waterproof paper and tied with black ribbon.

The cold metal of the gun seemed to burn into the flesh of my hand and I dropped it quickly onto the table and turned away to sit at the desk. Field Marshal Haig gazed at me with unquenchable confidence as I slit open the envelope.

It was shocking bad manners on your part, Adrian, not to answer my note, but I'll give you the benefit of the doubt and assume you never received it. I'm feeling rather dicky and have to make sure you get this package before my number comes up. Don't think it's my gift for posterity or anything of that kind. It's simply that I must tell someone so that my slate is wiped clean when I'm called to pass muster at the pearly gates. And you're the only one of the family left.

I wrote it all down a long time ago while the details were still fresh in my mind and added the ending later. Then, when your mother came to me as a secretary, I asked her to type it out. She and Fred Barnes were the only ones who ever knew the whole story and I made them swear never to tell anyone else, not even your father. But it isn't a story, Adrian. It's the truth and I've lived with it on my conscience all my life and now I've got to rid myself of it before I die. It will all seem ancient history to you—and yet, if it hadn't happened . . .

The next few lines were heavily scored, illegible, and the handwriting which followed, strong and clear till now, became weaker, agitated, harder to decipher.

I need to say one thing more. I'm truly sorry we had that misunderstanding which caused you to leave this house.

Your mother was no weaker than the rest of us. She was a fine woman, strong. But I was still angry that she'd accused me of being responsible for your father's death and that's why I spoke as I did. I fear that men are often angered by unpleasant truths. Forgive me, Adrian.

It was signed with his full name followed by his rank and decorations in brackets, and then there was a postscript, perhaps added the next day because the handwriting was stronger, clearly legible once more.

I don't know why I kept the revolver nor why I tried to give it to you. An unnecessay reminder of guilt and a useless attempt to escape from same, I suppose. I leave you to decide what to do with it as well as what I have written. Soon, God willing, neither will concern me any longer.

As a young officer I was taught to finish unpleasant company orders with some sort of a joke. So, over to you, as the frightened soldier said when he threw the grenade.

I remember untying the black ribbon, peeling away the rustling waterproof paper, taking out the thick wads of closely written, fading brown-inked pages, each with its neatly typed counterpart, and starting to read. Then nothing else until Miss Wilkins woke me in the morning and chastised me for sleeping in a chair in the study when she'd been to all the trouble of preparing a bed upstairs. Nothing else, that is, except for every word my mother had typed from my grandfather's original manuscript. She had altered the names of a few people, removed those of the regiments, simplified the military jargon, corrected some of the grammar. Edited the original, in fact, rewritten it without changing chronology or facts.

I said good-bye to Miss Wilkins, no longer a witch, just an ordinary person whose beginnings had been even less auspicious than my own, thanked her for being so good to my grandfather.

"He's been good to me," she said. "You'll never know how good."

But now, I did.

Then I found Fred's grave and said good-bye to him. The headstone bore an inscription identical to that of my grandfather's:

The peace of God
from Whom
no secrets are hid

Back in London I read my grandfather's manuscript again. At the foot of the final page of my mother's typed version he had written, Well done, Christine—no complaints.

She had given it a title: *The General's Narrative*.

I remembered what Richard had said. Christine always wanted to be a writer. Perhaps, even then, she'd been thinking of possible publication. Perhaps my grandfather had too.

I put an advertisement in the personal columns of *The Times* and the *Daily Telegraph*, added my telephone number.

GOLGOTHA. January, 1919.
Writer urgently requires information.
Please contact Adrian Garrard . . .

PART 2

THE GENERAL'S NARRATIVE

CHAPTER 4

Every story, Katherine used to tell me, should have a proper beginning, a point of departure. Mine is not one in the fictional sense although for a long time I had schooled myself to disguise facts in order to sustain hope, practiced self-delusion in the cause of self-survival. Such necessities were born of war. There is no further need for them now, no reason to exaggerate or minimize. The truth then, a true story. I can be precise as to its starting point. One A.M. on the morning of June 7th, 1917, in a forward trench outside Ypres, pinned down, as that whole blood-soaked salient had been for three years, by the massed German artillery on the commanding heights of Messines Ridge. Major John Richardson had been summoned to a briefing at battalion headquarters and I was temporarily in command.

"Special brew," Sergeant Wilkins said and handed me a tin mug. "Can't taste the bloody tea."

Our senior NCO had his own mysterious means of obtaining extra supplies of alcohol, and I had learned not to question them, just to be grateful. The whisky tasted excellent, warming.

A meat porter in Spitalfields before the war, George Wilkins had joined the colors, he told Richardson, to escape from the smell of dead meat. John had promoted him to lance corporal on the spot. Anyone with that sense of humor, he claimed, deserved nothing less. It exactly matched his own.

Wilkins had stayed close beside me the first time I went into action a year previously. "Don't waste your time praying, sir. God's got His hands full listening to terrified Jerries. Shoot them while they're still wondering if He's heard."

He'd seen me through my initial experience of mustard gas too, stopping in the drifting yellow clouds to check my mask, his voice echoing through his own. "Better than a London pea-souper. Buggers off as soon as the wind changes." I owed much to George Wilkins.

"God bless America," I said and drained the last dregs of the mug.

Two months previously the United States had declared war on Germany, and officers were encouraged to remind their men of the good news on all possible occasions.

Wilkins grinned. "Better come late than never come at all, as the actress said to the bishop. They're fine blokes in a scrap though. I got a mate in the flying corps. Keeps on about some Yank volunteer outfit with a fancy name."

"The Lafayette Squadron," I said.

"That's them. Fight like fucking tigers, my mate says." He turned abruptly as we heard a shout from the communication trench. "CO's coming back," he said. "Stand by for the blasphemy."

John Richardson hated HQ briefings. You came into contact with staff officers and could get polluted. In his book they were all expensively trained to be homicidal maniacs. But this time it was different. He actually looked happy.

"At last," he said, "a general who isn't a raving lunatic. D'you remember meeting old Mafeking, Adrian?"

Once, in another world, General Sir Herbert Plumer had led the Rhodesian relief force into that beleaguered town. I remembered him well. At the Bailleul railhead that spring he'd inspected our regiment on its way back into the line. With his white hair, potbelly, drooping walrus moustache and receding chin, he'd resembled the sort of benevolent uncle who chooses to remain in the background of family photographs yet never fails to provide, as presents, the most spectacular surprises.

It seemed he was about to provide one now.

"He's decided we'll never take the bloody ridge by direct assault, so he's going to blow it up instead," Richardson said.

"Blow it up?" Wilkins said. "What with? Hot air?"

Richardson explained. For a year now Plumer had been using

sappers and specially recruited miners to burrow eight thousand yards under German positions between Messines and Hill 60 where some had heard the voices of enemy tunneling parties digging alongside them in the opposite direction. But they hadn't been detected. Old Mafeking's latest surprise, nineteen huge mines, six thousand tons of high explosive planted deep beneath the churned mud of the surface, would, with luck, remain just that.

"When are they going to explode them?" I asked.

Richardson looked at his watch. "In precisely one hundred and twenty-five minutes from now. Ten past three this morning. We get a grandstand view, then comes the barrage, and then . . ."

"Us," Wilkins said.

"That's right," said John Richardson. "Let's go and tell the men."

We got our grandstand view at the exact moment promised in the program. The whole of the visible world before us erupted in a gigantic sheet of flame, and through swirls of black smoke we saw the darker shapes of guns, the torn twisting bodies of men, jagged chunks of the earth itself, rise up toward the sky, hang there for a moment, then fall back into the heaving chaos below.

"Previous clients accustomed to sleeping in the basement," Richardson said as the barrage roared overhead, "have now been reunited with more recent arrivals on the ground floor."

He liked to make that sort of joke before going over the top, a superstition perhaps, a kind of nugatory life insurance. Within twelve hours we had taken seven thousand terrified prisoners, and what remained of the Messines Ridge with its scattered plenitude of dead was in our hands.

And then we waited. Barely six miles ahead on another ridge stood the village of Passchendaele, Field Marshal Haig's magic key which would unlock the doors to the Belgian channel ports, justify, if justification were possible, the long bitter struggle to hold the Ypres salient. Passchendaele, Haig's talisman for glory. But we waited. For two months, while the sun shone and the politicians and the generals argued, we made no move.

And then at last, on July 31st came the order to advance. And with it came the rain. The Menin Road, Sanctuary, Polygon, Glencorse Woods, the unceasing uncaring downpour, the obscene sucking mud, the uncounted uncountable dead. In six weeks we had advanced five miles. The newspapers hailed a great victory.

Perhaps I was too hasty in selecting my starting point. Dawn on October 13th, a month before my twenty-second birthday, would have been better. That was the morning we launched our attack on the talisman, on Passchendaele. Our assault trench was no more than an irregular row of shell holes linked together by ditches dug out of the surrounding quagmire, strengthened where possible by hastily laid duckboards, the parapets close-packed mud, the firesteps old ammunition boxes, sometimes corpses. In each the water level was never less than a couple of feet. Passchendaele was very close, but we couldn't see it because it no longer existed as a village, only one more ruin in a ruined wasteland, a circled dot on wet and bloodstained maps.

The men were given cocoa liberally laced with rum. Richardson and I drank brandy. It was supposed to stimulate courage, confidence, before an attack. Increasingly, it seemed to be having the opposite effect on John. "Bloody senseless murder," he muttered. "I'm not going this time."

In the past few weeks he'd become more of an automaton than a man capable of rational thought, a robot whose sole function was to kill or be killed. He'd go because there was nothing else he could do until his body, like his mind, was blown to pieces. "Haig's mad," he said loudly. "Except for old Mafeking, they're all fucking mad."

I looked along the ditch to see if any of the men had heard. The nearest was Wilkins. In charge of the digging party, he hadn't slept for twenty-four hours, but he was making up for it now, leaning against the mud wall, a fat well-fed rat clawing up his arm toward his face. I lunged at it and it dropped heavily into the slime. Wilkins did not wake.

"Gentlemen of England now abed," Richardson said. "If you've got any bloody sense, stay there. You might live through the day."

He was killed ten minutes later, his body sawn in half by machine-gun bullets. I saw it happen.

"Just time for the lice game," he said. "Bet you a fiver."

The rules were simple. Whoever picked the greater number of lice off the other's clothing was the winner. Those plucked from the skin counted double. It passed the time at tense moments and was, I suppose, a small gesture toward cleanliness.

Our contest was brought to an abrupt end by a rushing roar overhead. Star shells flared in the grey sky, the mud heaved. The barrage had begun. Whistles sounded all along the waterlogged ditch. Wilkins woke up and yelled, "Stand to!"

"Damn," Richardson said mildly, "I was winning by a distance."

On either side of us men clambered on to the makeshift firesteps, their heads bent beneath the level of the parapet. A fanciful person might have imagined they were praying and perhaps a few were. I heard a plopping sound below me and looked down to see if I'd dropped some part of my equipment. Wilkins's rat had been joined by several others, and they were all sloshing around in the mire, biting eagerly at something in the mud wall. There's plenty of flesh to be found on a human hand, the promise of more to come for a rat with experience. This lot had plenty. The trench had been dug on fought-over ground and, as always, in a hurry. Richardson saw them, too.

"Bless them," he said, "for they shall inherit the earth."

He grinned at me, white teeth gleaming. He always carried a tin of tooth powder in his pack.

"Not bloody going this time," he said, then stood up straight and yelled, waving his right arm in a great sweeping arc toward Passchendaele. We followed him as he scrambled over the parapet.

Like all such attacks, I don't remember that one with any particular clarity. If anyone did, he'd probably never take part in another. Easier to be arrested and shot by one's own side, gas mask reversed over the head, padre wishing godspeed, all the ritual trimmings. You only remember disconnected fragments, chaotic, without pattern or order. Two enemies, one trying to shoot, the other trying to drown you. A man falls in your path, howling like a dog as the mud sucks him down, chokes him into perpetual silence. You mustn't stop, mustn't falter. That's what they want, a sitting target. You swear at the churning, clinging slime, drive forward, shout with sudden unbelieving delight as your boots strike a patch of drier ground. Running now, weaving, returning their fire. The top half of Richardson's torso flying through the air, striking you in the face, blood blinding you. You can't see but you keep running, shouting, firing. Then suddenly you're down and all movement stops like a jammed cine film. You're still screaming, but now it's different. It's because of the pain, and when you try to get up, your legs won't move. You don't know where you are. All you know is that you're alone and probably going to die. When you stop screaming and look up, the sky is dark and you can't hear the guns any more, only the sound of someone moaning softly. It takes a few moments before you realize it's yourself.

I must have passed out, lain there all day. When I came to, it was night, the rain sheeting down, a curtain of dirty crystals, each one faintly lit by pale moonlight. Perhaps it was that other enemy, the rain, which had brought me back to consciousness and I remembered something Richardson had said at Polygon Wood.

"God's tears," he'd said.

I tried to shout for stretcher bearers, knowing they must have long since passed, that they never stopped for those they believed dead, that my voice was too weak to reach them anyway.

The pain had gone. Slowly I lifted one arm then the other, flexed my fingers, felt the mud squelch in my cold hands. I breathed in carefully, then more deeply. No difficulty. My lungs, at least, seemed to be in full working order. Then I tried to move my legs. Nothing happened. No discomfort, no sensation, nothing. They no longer appeared to exist. But by raising myself just a few inches on my elbows I could see them, one ankle crossed neatly over the other as though in sleep. They were not asleep though, they were dead. I let my head sink back and felt tears on my cheeks, warm against the chill of the rain. I had never prayed that I might live, only the soldier's prayer that if death were to come, it would come quickly. Perhaps Richardson had made the same plea, and I envied him its answer. Then I began speaking out loud, addressing God with urgency, apologizing for that unworthy thought, begging Him, at last, for my own life. Fear brings many to the faith, and I'd bet that by the end the Flanders tally exceeded that of all the medieval inquisitors.

If wounded, they taught you at Sandhurst, if immobilized, do not give in, do not let go. Use your eyes, look around you, select some object of interest, fix it in your mind, concentrate, keep hold. I looked around. If this were to be my last sight of the world, it was not one of which I wished to keep hold but only to forget.

I seemed to be lying on some sort of comparatively solid mound in the sodden earth. My palms felt the jagged edges of what could once have been bricks or cement. My elevated resting place afforded an interrupted view of the surroundings. Black mud pitted with shell holes, torn trunks of trees, torn trunks of men, a vision of hell, the death of all living things, desolate, damned.

I no longer knew the direction of our own positions nor those of the enemy but this seemed unimportant. There was only one enemy left now, and a part of me longed for his victory, my release. They called the place No Man's Land and it was well named.

The rain stopped. I watched a dark cloud pass across the moon to be replaced by thinner wispy veils of grey.

I shall never feel peace in the moonlight again, only fear, because it was then that I saw the first of them.

It appeared over the lip of a crater, crouching on all fours, its black head twitching rapidly from side to side, sensing danger, scenting prey. Then it began to crawl through the mud toward me.

In a nightmare you can sometimes compel your eyes to open, regain the real world, drive away the horror. I closed mine and strove to do the same. When I opened them again, the creature was only fifteen yards away, but now it had stopped, its head bent forward over one of the twisted corpses, its darting forepaws tearing at the dead man's clothing. Through a red mist of terror one conscious thought emerged. My revolver. If I couldn't kill it before it got to me, I would kill myself. I scrabbled at the holster. It was empty. The gun must have been in my hand when I was hit. God knew where it was now. I jerked my head desperately trying to see it and heard a dreadful baying sound like the howl of a wolf, then another and another. Three more creatures were climbing out of the crater, dropping down into the slime. The first turned, snarled an answer, leapt onto the corpse to claim it, twitched its head again, seeking further quarry.

Then it came lumbering straight toward me.

I heard the sickening sucking sound as its legs drove it closer and closer through the clinging mud and could not look. And then I heard laughter. Harsh, grating, wild, only just recognizable, but laughter.

I forced my eyes open.

The creature had risen onto its rear legs and, still bent forward, was clutching my revolver between its forepaws. Only they weren't paws, they were earth-blackened hands, and the creature was not an animal but a man, his head shrouded in a cowl of filthy sacking, his clothes blackened rags. He looked behind him, gave a hoarse bark of triumph, and I knew enough German to recognize it as a word. Its English equivalent echoed back across the desolation from two of the others crouched over preys of their own.

"Gun! Gun!"

I lay still, feigning death. The clawlike hands ripped at my clothes. Perhaps this was death.

Without warning, the world exploded, the sky flamed, the broken bricks beneath me trembled. Another barrage saluting another dawn.

With horror and relief I saw the four dark shapes crawl back to the lip of the crater, the mud rising to embrace and hide them.

Then, suddenly, blackness, merciful oblivion.

I woke screaming. They hadn't gone. They were still there, surrounding me, and I was somehow suspended between them, flat on my back, the sky tilting above me, unable to move, helpless, their prisoner on a journey into Hades. Somewhere in the distance I could hear a dirgelike voice, raucous, tuneless.

> The world wasn't made in a day
> And Eve didn't ride in a bus,
> Most of the world's in a sandbag
> And the rest of it's plastered on us.

I screamed more loudly to try and drown the sound but it was useless.

A mud-stained face swam into view close above my own, blotting out the sky, filling what remained of the world.

"Don't try talking, sir. No breath for more than a whisper. Can't hear a word."

I stopped screaming, stared up at the face.

"Sergeant Wilkins here," it said. "We've got you on a stretcher. Lie still. Back home in no time."

The face twisted away and I heard its angry shout.

"Stop your bloody singing, for Christ's sake, or I'll shoot you myself."

The fury of that voice was the last thing I remembered till I came to in the advanced field dressing station.

* * *

"First Mr. Richardson, now you," Wilkins said cheerfully. "Things go on like this, I'll be a bloody officer next week."

I wanted to tell him what I'd seen out there in the moonlight of No Man's Land but hadn't the strength for more than a few garbled words.

"The MO's coming now," Wilkins said. "Only been up here a few days. Don't you go giving him no stuff about wild animals— scare the wits out of him that would."

I tried to speak again, to tell them.

"Quiet now," the MO said. "I'll do the talking."

He looked alarmingly young, slightly embarrassed, and already very weary.

"You're my first officer casualty," he said.

"Don't balls it up then," Wilkins growled. "Been lying out there twenty-four fucking hours this gentleman has."

"My name's Selfridge," the MO said as he cut away my trousers. "Same as the store in Oxford Street, makes it easy to remember."

I didn't know whether he was chattering to keep me quiet or himself awake. Either way I wished he'd stop. I had more important things to say.

"Whatever you do," he said suddenly, "please don't try to move your legs." As jokes went it was a classic, a real gem. I looked up into his sweating face and laughed out loud.

"Hold him still," he shouted at Wilkins and turned away to fill his syringe. It seemed to take a long time, and I couldn't check the laughter.

"One's heard about it, of course," Selfridge said to Wilkins, "but one doesn't really believe it till one sees it."

"Heard about what?" Wilkins asked impatiently, gripping my shoulders.

"Their courage," whispered Selfridge. "The way they laugh in the face of . . ."

He plunged the needle into my arm and I heard no more.

The next thing I remember was an orderly looking down at me. He carried something that looked like raw meat in a metal dish. My legs were firmly strapped to another stretcher.

"There's an ambulance due," he said. "It'll take you back to the railhead. Your sergeant's waiting to say good-bye."

God knows how Wilkins had managed to get there, but he was a man with his own sense of priorities and his private means of satisfying them without being seen to flout authority. In any case this was no time to ask. I had more important information to give him.

"Listen, Wilkins, before you found me last night—"

He laughed. "Not last night, Mr. Garrard. Two days ago."

I blinked at him, trying to focus. He held a tin of bully beef in one hand, a carton of Woodbines in the other. Farewell to his CO combined with a visit to the canteen. An experienced soldier. Practical.

"Young Selfridge took a bullet out of your hip. Never thought he'd even be able to find it by the look of him."

"Listen, sergeant—"

"He left another where it was. Said he hadn't got no more time. Cheeky young bugger."

I took a deep breath. "I'm giving you an order, Wilkins."

"What's that, sir?"

"Stop talking."

"Very good, sir."

I told him then, all of it. The creatures from the crater, the way they'd splashed through the mud on all fours, the rape of the corpses, the icy feel of the claw-hands on my body, the obscene scuttle for safety when the barrage began.

"I thought they were animals," I said, "but they weren't. They were men."

Wilkins's face seemed to age suddenly. I'd seen the same look on those of men who'd been forced to stay on in the line because a relied-upon relief had failed to materialize. A Dorian Gray effect but not the result of dissipation, simply recognition of a horror past bearing.

"Soldiers?" he asked quietly. "Them as just couldn't take it so . . . ?"

He didn't finish the question.

"Demented bastards," I said.

"God Almighty," he whispered. "God Almighty's fucking truth."

"I want you to tell the CO, Wilkins."

"CO's gone to glory, sir."

"The new one then."

He looked doubtful.

"Prissy young sod, sir. Straight out from Camberley. Stupid with it. Thinks I'm taking a message to brigade HQ this minute."

"Tell him, Wilkins," I said. "He'll know what to do."

"Only if he can find it in his blasted training manual," Wilkins said.

"It's another order, sergeant."

"Understood, Mr. Garrard. Best be getting back now. Someone's got to point Percy Bates in the direction of the enemy."

"Percy Bates?"

"The prissy sod. That's his name. Don't let none of those Le Touquet quacks fuck you up."

He stopped at the entrance to the canvas tent, looked back.

"Might let the nurses have a go, though. Good luck."

Of course the ambulance didn't arrive at the expected time. Few ever did. The roads shown on their maps had usually disappeared before they began their journey.

Selfridge carried a wooden stool over to my stretcher and sat down.

"Five minutes' break," he said. "I need it. Suppose I should give you a final examination."

I thanked him for extracting at least one of the bullets. He explained that the other was very close to the base of my spine.

"They'll remove that back at Le Touquet. It'll be a tricky job but they've got all the facilities and they'll do their stuff. After that it's up to you. Take your time. Do what they tell you. Don't get impatient."

I realized he was warning me that if I did, I'd probably end up half paralyzed for life.

"Don't worry," he said. "They're good surgeons."

"You're not so bad yourself," I said.

He shrugged. "Never wanted to be one. Psychiatry's my game. But they were screaming for men to mend bodies, so I did my patriotic duty. I'll get back to the mind after the war, if I survive it."

He looked as though he would. Wilkins, on the other hand,

might not, might even be killed before he could pass on my message to his new CO.

I decided to tell Selfridge everything just as I'd told it to him. There was no harm in making doubly sure. He listened intently.

"Animals, you say?"

"They looked like animals, but they weren't. They were men. At least they had been men."

"And they just—appeared?"

"From the crater," I said. "Out of the ground."

"I see," Selfridge said thoughtfully. "And you think they must have been living down there beneath the surface like . . . like troglodytes?"

I nodded, pleased at his quick understanding.

"God knows how many. I only saw four. There may be hundreds—thousands."

He peered closely at my face, shining a small torch into each of my eyes, completing his examination.

"You believe me, don't you?" I asked. I was to ask the same question many more times in many different places but did not know it then. All I knew was that the answer was desperately important.

Selfridge slipped the torch back into his pocket.

"You've told me what you saw," he said gently. "Who am I to disbelieve it?"

There was a sudden commotion outside. The ambulance had arrived.

Selfridge patted me on the shoulder. "Best not dwell on it," he said briskly. "The memory'll soon fade."

In the Stroombeek Valley near Passchendaele, two men in blackened rags crawled, one behind the other, along an underground passage hewn deep in the earth, climbed slowly and painfully upward through a sloping tunnel, part of whose jagged walls had once belonged to an intricate network of trenches and dugouts, long since reduced to chaotic rubble. They emerged into the cold darkness of the night, crouched there on all fours, their heads twitching from side to side, listening for dangers, scenting prey.

The first man's name was Shaw, and he called his companion the Marksman because he had once been trained as a sniper and still remembered how to use a rifle. He carried one now. The Marksman had tried calling Shaw the Wolf because of his sloping forehead, his thin face, and the way he bared his teeth when angry. But Shaw prided himself on remembering his own name and would accept no other. So the Marksman, like everyone else, called him Shaw.

They were searching for food, for the dead who carried it.

In their subterranean community these were two of the leaders.

CHAPTER 5

The casino at Le Touquet, the great chandeliers muffled now in huge dust sheets, static grey-white clouds floating above the rows of closely packed beds, their glamour, like that of the roulette and chemin de fer tables, banished for the duration. But the wits still protested *rien ne va plus* when told that a further operation was necessary, and in the heavy ether-laden atmosphere, gambling of a more basic, grimmer kind had its place. The medical staff was compelled to act as the croupiers, and bets were laid on which of three cards they would deal to us, the wounded. They would not decide who was to leave the hospital or who would remain because in the end everyone would go. They decided, simply, the fashion of their going. Three cards, three options. An ambulance to Boulogne and England, a train to the railhead and the front line, a coffin to the nearest graveyard and the Last Post.

Most of the doctors and nurses had been there a long time, a few from the very beginning. They had learned to dispense, along with the anesthetics and medicaments, the precious gift of hope, and when that ran out, a gentle understanding, the bestowal of dignity.

There may have been no real angels at Mons, but there were plenty of both sexes at Le Touquet. They cleaned up the site of the first bullet, removed the second, and by the end of February, 1918, I knew for sure that I was destined to draw the lucky card, a ticket to the haven known as Blighty.

In the meantime I obeyed orders by lying on my back, gathering strength for the journey, and staring up at the dust sheet clouds. The monotony of this overhead view was enlivened as often as possible by the presence of a white sheet spread horizontally and tautly between the rigid stems of four shrouded chandeliers. On to it were projected, vertically, moving pictures, the films of such as Charlie Chaplin, the Keystone Cops. This cinematic innovation was principally the work of our senior ward sister, Staff Nurse Katherine Poole. She had come out to France in the early days, a passenger aboard Sir Thomas Lipton's yacht, the *Erin*, a girl of barely eighteen, eager for adventure, determined not to miss this one, the biggest of them all. Adventure had long since given place to ceaseless grinding routine, but Katherine's spirit had refused to be defeated by it. She waged a determined campaign to ensure that like pain, boredom, if it could not be removed altogether, must at least be alleviated. The overhead cinema shows were one of its most spectacular results. Her father, she told me, had supplied both equipment and technical advice.

She told me much else besides. Her parents lived in the village of Boscastle on the northeast coast of Cornwall where her father was the local general practitioner. The Cornish, it seemed, did not share the national reverence for food rationing. The wars of men prevented neither chickens from laying nor pigs from breeding. If they, the residents of that other part of the kingdom across the river, wished to deprive themselves of eggs and bacon for breakfast, that was their affair. West of the Tamar the gifts of nature were not to be wasted even if they had pronounced them illicit. There was even, whispered Katherine, clotted cream for tea. After leaving school, she had helped her father in his small nursing home where he had installed in a former cowshed the first X-ray apparatus seen in the Duchy. The villagers, she solemnly assured me, would utter prayers for deliverance before entering its presence. She spoke of childhood walks beside the magic streams of the Valency valley where she longed to rediscover the drinking goblet lost there by Thomas Hardy and his Emma during the briefly happy days of their courtship; of picnics on the broad sands of Trebarwith; of visits to the ruined castle at Tintagel. Some day, she maintained, King Arthur would return. She laughed when she said this, but I know that she half-believed it. There was once a Camelot. There would be again.

Her eyes were the blue-grey color of Cornish seas, and when she smiled, they shone and sparkled as even those waters may do in the warmth of a summer sun. She smiled very frequently, not offering the kindly but semi-automatic cheer of those who nurse the sick, but from a natural deep-seated sense of enjoyment in life itself. I remember the first time I saw her long blond hair, normally concealed in a bun beneath her cap. Officially off-duty, she had come running into the ward with fresh supplies of morphia needed for an unexpected new batch of casualties. As she left, she had stopped beside my bed for a moment and, putting her hand to the nape of her neck, had lifted the glistening plume into its usual position on top of her head.

"*Most* unnurselike," she had said and laughed.

That was the moment when I knew for certain that I was falling in love.

Charlie Chaplin wove his magic spell on the sheet above us. Katherine sat on a chair at the end of my bed, her head arched back, laughing up at him.

"How wonderful," she said. "The chance to make people happy."

In the semidarkness I watched the smooth white line of her throat and marveled at its beauty.

The vast ward was suddenly flooded with light, returning to reality as the film flickered to its end. Katherine straightened her head slowly so that she was looking directly at me, and I was shocked to see tears on her cheeks.

"So silly," she said quickly. "I was hoping it would last forever."

I wanted to tell her that one day it would. Not the film, the chance of happiness, given and received. I wanted to tell her that I loved her. But I did neither because she brushed the tears away before anyone else could notice them and spoke briskly to me and to those on either side.

"Shan't be tucking you in tonight, boys, my free evening. A special dinner."

"The lucky captain from Etaples again," said a lieutenant without rancor. "Whole in body and, let us hope, clean in spirit."

"Contrary to army belief," Katherine said primly, "not all military police are monsters. Some are actually quite human."

A stab of unreasoning jealousy made me try to sit up, an absurd attempt to detain her.

"Why's it so special?"

"My twenty-first birthday," she said and put her hand on my chest, pushing me back against the pillows.

"Don't try to rush things," she added quietly. "Not till we're agreed it's the right moment."

But the others heard her. "Sister Poole should be appointed chief adviser to GHQ forthwith," the lieutenant said.

I joined in the general laughter as she blew us all a farewell kiss. When I can walk again, I thought, that will be the right moment. Then I shall ask her to marry me.

It took another four weeks, and I was still using crutches when I invited Katherine to have dinner at Le Touquet's best remaining restaurant, Le Chat Bleu. I remember the date, March 23rd, 1918.

"Would you mind if Roy joined us?" she asked.

"Who's Roy?"

"Roy Meadows, the monster redcap. The captain from Etaples."

I was furious, filled with black despair.

"I'd mind very much," I said. "Very much indeed."

"That's a pity. He's most anxious to talk to you. Sent over a special message."

"Bugger his messages," I shouted. "Have you any idea *why* I've arranged this dinner?"

"An inkling," she said.

"I want to marry you, for Christ's sake," I said, and I was still shouting. She looked at me for what seemed like minutes, staring into my eyes, then turned away to gaze out across the casino gardens, probably once green and smooth, now churned into a brown morass by countless feet, the tires of wheeling ambulances. We were standing at the top of the entrance steps, and I dreaded maneuvering down them on the crutches, dreaded far more what her next words would be.

"Are you sure you mean that?" she said.

"Of course I bloody well mean it."

I hadn't intended to swear again, but it had assumed the quality of an insurance against disappointment, a kind of refuge.

She turned back to me very slowly, and once again I saw tears on her cheeks, but now her eyes were bright and smiling.

"Whatever you do," she said, "don't think of adding to the

delicacy of that proposal by trying to go down on one knee. The crutches wouldn't stand it."

"Katherine, please . . ."

"I accept," she said. "I want to marry you. I want that more than anything in the world."

I took her in my arms and kissed her. Not once, many times. In the end she had to prop me against the door frame while she retrieved the fallen crutches from the bottom of the steps. Then we went out to dinner.

Roy Meadows had sandy-colored hair, a small wisp of moustache to match. He wore plain clothes, tweed jacket, grey trousers. "Thought you might prefer mufti," he said. "Some people don't like being seen out with my lot. Understandable, I suppose."

Katherine had announced our engagement as soon as we arrived. "Reported to the arm of the law," she'd said. "That makes it official."

Meadows had offered congratulations, ordered champagne, and apologized profusely for making it a crowd of three when the occasion clearly called for only two. I liked him, but on that particular night I suppose I'd have liked almost anyone.

"You wanted to talk to me," I said.

"Wilkins," Meadows said. "Sergeant Wilkins."

The automatic shock which neither time nor repetition could ever quite still. The feeling of useless loss, the sense of bitterness. Another death. Another friend gone, this time a close one. It didn't occur to me to wonder why an officer of the military police in Etaples should come to be the bearer of such news.

"Where was he killed?" I asked.

Meadows shook his head, spoke in a series of staccato bursts as though anxious to make bad news clear but get it over and done with as rapidly as possible.

"He's in the stockade at Etaples, detention camp. Been there four months. Under close arrest. Accused of striking an officer. Admits it. Field general court-martial tomorrow. Foregone conclusion. Unless . . ." He paused, a machine gun suddenly run dry of ammunition. I stared at him, unable to take it in. Meadows took a deep breath, reloaded, fired off more information.

"Thought you were back in Blighty, didn't realize you were

here till a couple of days ago. Katherine mentioned your name. Same name Wilkins gave me. Thought—best have a talk."

We sat there finishing the rest of our celebratory champagne and talked. Meadows did most of it.

Wilkins had apparently made some sort of report to a Lieutenant Percy Bates. The lieutenant had refused to believe it, accused him of panic, alarmism, spreading false rumors to the detriment of morale. Wilkins said the report had originated with me. Bates called him a liar. Wilkins insisted. I had given him orders to pass it on. In that case, Bates told him, I was a liar and an alarmist, too. At which point Wilkins punched him on the jaw, knocking him to the ground. There were several witnesses to the assault, and their signed statements had been collected by Bates and forwarded together with his own as per regulations. It had all taken time. That was one reason Wilkins had been in captivity for four months. The other was that finding officers qualified and willing to sit on a court-martial was always a slow process. From the beginning few had ever shown much keenness. After three and a half years of war, there were fewer still.

"Did Wilkins tell you what was in the report?" I asked.

"The charge is striking a superior officer—"

"Did he *tell* you?"

Meadows glanced quickly at Katherine, took a final sip of champagne, leaned toward me.

"Yes," he said quietly, "he did."

"And you believed him?"

He sat back in his chair again, fingers twirling the stem of his empty glass.

"Look, Garrard, the point of all this is that when you've been in charge of prisoners as long as I have, you develop a sixth sense about them. Either they're no good, deserve what's coming to them, or they're basically fine soldiers who've run into a bit of bad luck. Straw and the camel's back." He put the glass down carefully on the tablecloth. "Your Sergeant Wilkins belongs to the second category."

It was the longest uninterrupted statement he'd made and I knew he meant every word of it.

"Will Bates be there tomorrow?"

"Unnecessary. Court has his sworn testimony and Wilkins has

already admitted guilt. Ten years' jail at least. Possibly . . ." He broke off, looked at Katherine.

"Death?" she asked quietly and Meadows nodded.

"Can't ever tell with members of a FGCM. Not volunteers, all detailed. Not trained, all laymen. Some automatically award the maximum sentence and leave it to the C in C to reduce it later if he wants. Unsatisfactory. Inhuman. Mad."

"Like the rest of this war," Katherine said.

I felt beside me for the first of the crutches. Rising from the dinner table was still a lengthy operation, requiring careful preparation.

"Unless—what?" I asked Meadows.

"Mitigating circumstances. Outside chance. Up to you."

"Can I see Wilkins now? Tonight?"

"Highly irregular," Meadows said and smiled for the first time since he'd toasted Katherine's and my future married bliss.

"Only five kilometers. Suggest we use my transport."

As we were leaving the restaurant, he asked Katherine if she'd mind coming with us.

"Professional capacity, nurse. Ease explanations to my chaps. Claim visit on medical grounds. All right?"

"Absolutely all right," Katherine said.

I knew the camp at Etaples, of course, the Bull Ring where troops arriving from England were trained for what lay ahead. If you survived the Bull Ring, they said, the trenches would seem like paradise. In some respects it was not wholly an exaggeration. But I was not prepared for the stockade itself. Huge ten-foot-high wooden stakes driven deep into the sandy soil, and inside that rigid perimeter two heavily woven barbed-wire entanglements, each at least twice the strength and thickness of anything ever seen in No Man's Land. The authorities had had plenty of time to build defenses here against escape by their own as yet legally innocent men, no shells, no machine guns to impede their painstaking work. The whole area was floodlit, guarded at every heavy gate by armed sentries. I wondered if any of those creatures I'd seen crawling from their crater in front of Passchendaele had known of this place. Had they perhaps consciously chosen that nether hell beneath the scarred battlefields rather than submit themselves to one constructed by their comrades in arms? Each man, I thought, has his

own breaking point, but having reached it, still his own interpreta-
tion of freedom and, somewhere beyond desperation, his own
choice. For the first time I experienced a trace of pity for those
crazed self-elected outcasts, a small stir of understanding, even
sympathy.

We passed through huddles of small brown tents, our safe
conduct guaranteed by Meadows's sharp passwords, brief explanations, stopped at one of the smallest of all.

"I'll stay outside with Katherine," he said to me. "Anyone asks
questions, you're a doctor, she's a nurse waiting for your instructions. Ten minutes. In you go."

A pretty improbable doctor, I thought, and bent low on my
crutches to enter through the canvas flap. The roof of the tent was
so low that I had to remain stooping inside it. I looked at the man
crouching on the dirty sand of the floor. His attitude resembled that
of a dog accustomed to whippings, but he twisted his head as he
heard me and gave a sort of warning snarl, still his own master, still
defiant.

"Hullo, Wilkins," I said.

He peered at me through the gloom, his fingers scrabbling for
something dark and shapeless on the ground. The thick stubble on
his face could not hide its prison pallor. Then he recognized me.

"God Almighty," he whispered.

I kept my eyes on the thing in his hand.

"What's that, sergeant?"

He grinned, saliva glinting on his bared teeth, and for a
horrifying moment I was reminded of the wolf face looming over
mine in the mud of Passchendaele. A different sort of prisoner
seeking a different means of survival.

"Sandbag," Wilkins said. "Small but useful. Last weapon left.
In here we call 'em thuds."

"No," I said sharply. "No more of that."

He let the thing drop from his fingers.

"You wouldn't know about it, sir, but I'm for the chop
tomorrow."

"I know all about it, Wilkins."

He went on speaking as though he hadn't heard me.

"Small enough to hide inside my shirt. Take it in with me. That
little bastard Bates'll be there. I'll get him. Christ, I'll get him."

"He won't be there," I said, and repeated it to make sure he'd understood.

Wilkins's whole body sagged, his face seemed to crumple. I had taken away the last surge of strength that was sustaining him. The promise of revenge.

"How d'you know that?" he whispered, and his voice was like that of a child, bewildered, abandoned, admitting finally to an overwhelming fear beyond its understanding.

I told him, and then what I proposed to do about it. It took every one of Meadows's allotted ten minutes, but by the time I'd finished, I was sure Wilkins had understood.

"One thing I just remembered, Mr. Garrard. After it happened, one of the lads told me Bates was talking to that MO when we come out of the line, the one that took out your bullet."

"Selfridge?"

"Yes. That's him."

Selfridge, the surgeon who had wanted to be a psychiatrist.

"What did they talk about?"

"Dunno, sir. P'r'aps it'll be in the little sod's report."

"Perhaps," I said.

Wilkins forced a grin.

"Ten ack emma in the morning," he said. "I'd ask you to stay the night only there ain't no spare room."

Meadows stuck his head through the flap.

"Padre's coming," he said and glanced quickly at Wilkins. "Routine visit."

"Do everything they can to cheer a man up in here," Wilkins said. The grin was still there but fear lurked in his eyes. I pushed the thud into the far corner with one of the crutches before leaving the tent.

Outside the stockade Meadows handed me a dog-eared copy of the *Manual of Military Law*, 1914 edition.

"Forewarned, forearmed," he said.

Then he drove us back to the casino, sitting alone in the front of his open truck, hands gripping the wheel, eyes constantly scanning the road on either side. Perhaps he was observing his own dictum, already establishing an alibi should higher authority later accuse him of using official transport for private purposes. He could say he was looking for escaped prisoners. Katherine and I held each other's hands in the back. She pointed at one of the houses in the main square of Etaples.

"That's where Napoleon and Marshal Ney stayed when they were planning their invasion of England," she said. "There's a plaque."

"The French like to advertise their failures," Meadows said to the steering wheel.

I remembered the detailed description, promulgated throughout our division in routine orders, of the execution of a soldier for desertion. Two of his friends had been blown to bits beside him by exploding shells, and he had pleaded that he no longer knew where he was or where he was going. It made no difference. When he faced the firing squad at dawn, he was just eighteen years old. Not only the French, I thought.

In the Stroombeek another black figure, anonymous in his rags, indistinguishable in the dark night from Shaw or the Marksman, scrambled up over the lip of a shell crater, and as they had done, became still and watchful, only his eyes moving like those of an animal, the hunted and the hunter. Then he began to move forward in a crawling lope toward the closest of the bodies.

Unlike Shaw, he had long since forgotten his own name but he could remember other things. A village in Austria called Lambach, a monastery, snatches of psalms and hymns he had sung there. Shaw had dubbed him the Shouter, and time had taught them to trust one another. He heard Shaw's distant questioning cry now and, after a moment, lifted his head from the corpse and answered it warily, careful not to shout too loudly. Their language was their own, belonging to neither's country, to none.

The Shouter was another of the leaders.

CHAPTER 6

The court consisted of a major, a captain and a subaltern. The major, who was also the president, had lost his right hand and experienced obvious difficulty writing with his left. The captain's cheeks were an unhealthy grey color, and he breathed in short grasping gasps. I recognized the symptoms. Gas poisoning. The fair-haired subaltern looked like a junior prefect at an English public school and blushed whenever one of the others glanced in his direction. He couldn't have been more than nineteen. All three gave the distinct impression that they would much prefer to be somewhere else, but none more so than the prosecuting officer, a lieutenant with a round kindly face and steel spectacles. He had no opposite number, no "prisoner's friend," no counsel for the defense.

Wilkins was conducting his own defense, in so far as a plea of guilty could be considered as such. Meadows and two of his redcaps sat behind him but took no part in the proceedings.

The lieutenant had opened with a half-hearted protest regarding the presence of Katherine and myself, but I had spent half the night studying Meadows's manual and was ready for it. Among many other things it stated that courts-martial should be open to the public, military or otherwise, providing there was sufficient space to accommodate them. In this instance there certainly was. We were in the gymnasium of the Bull Ring, its wall bars suggesting the torture of the rack, its dangling ropes a scaffold. The manual had nothing to say on the subject of wounded personnel being accompanied by their medical attendants, but I made great play of standing up on my crutches to address the president, taking care to look straight at the black leather glove covering his artificial hand. He overruled the objections, and Katherine in her hospital uniform was provided with a chair next to mine at the side of the court. She had insisted on obtaining leave to be there, and I thought I saw Meadows smile as she sat down, but couldn't be sure.

Looking considerably relieved that there could be no further conceivable causes for delay, the lieutenant launched into the case for the prosecution. He presented it clearly and concisely, obviously anxious to complete an unpleasant job as quickly as possible and then, probably, have a good lunch and forget it.

While in the front line, the accused had made a report to his commanding officer. The officer had regarded it as a fabrication deliberately designed to undermine morale and had refused to believe it. The accused claimed that he had been told to make the report by a previous CO, now wounded and out of the line. The officer had refused to believe that either. The accused had then struck the officer. Details of times, names, and places were before each member of the court together with sworn statements by the officer himself and several independent witnesses. The accused had been made aware of them. The entire presentation would have taken less than five minutes had it not been for constant lengthy pauses while the major laboriously and painfully noted down the spoken words with his left hand. As it was, it took more than twenty.

The court shuffled the sheafs of papers on the table in front of them, the captain holding his at a distance from his face as though any closer proximity might further impair his breathing. The subaltern glanced through his with distaste as though being forced to read an unfavorable end-of-term report. They had all seen them before anyway. Finally, the major dropped his onto the table, held them down with his false hand, looked at Wilkins.

"Does the accused plead guilty or not guilty?" he asked.

"Guilty," Wilkins said.

The captain snorted, perhaps a physical necessity rather than a comment, and the subaltern stared fixedly at the floor.

"You understand the gravity of the charge?" asked the major. His voice sounded weary but only faintly surprised.

"Yes, sir," said Wilkins.

"Anything further you'd like to add? Any—er—mitigating circumstances?"

Wilkins's eyes flickered briefly toward me then looked the major straight in the face.

"If the same thing happened again," he said, "I wouldn't act no different."

The captain took a deep rasping breath, spoke for the first time.

"Are you saying you'd repeat the offense? Strike an officer?" He leaned back in his chair temporarily exhausted by the effort.

"Not any officer," Wilkins said. "Captain Bates, if he was to say again what he said then."

There was a terrible silence broken only by the rustling of papers as the court quickly reminded themselves of Bates's identity. The major looked up at the prosecuting officer.

"Captain Bates is unable to be present in person?"

"Captain Bates was killed in action two months ago, sir," said the lieutenant, trying, to give him his due, not to make it sound too much like playing a trump card.

The major nodded, rose stiffly, pushing himself up from the table with his left hand, seeming to lift the other as an afterthought, something which did not rightfully belong to him and might just as well have been left where it was.

"The court will now consider its findings," he said. "The court is . . ."

"I request permission to call a witness for the defense, sir," Wilkins said loudly. I'd rehearsed him in the phrase the night before and he delivered it with all the panache of a trained king's counsel.

"Quite impossible," the lieutenant said before the major could speak. "The president has declared the court closed."

"He hasn't actually," the subaltern said unexpectedly but very distinctly. He looked across at the major, his face scarlet. "You hadn't actually completed the declaration, sir. I mean fair's fair, isn't it?"

The major glared at the subaltern, then at Wilkins, then at me. I think he was already beginning to suspect. He placed his false hand back on the table and sat down.

"What witness?" He was still looking at me. So was Wilkins.

"Captain Garrard, sir," he said, and pointed in my direction. "My old CO. Him Mr. Bates called a liar."

A further silence, complete save for a further anxious rustling of papers.

"Captain Garrard is so named in the relevant statements, sir," said the lieutenant. If, as I suspect, he was simply trying to save time, he suceeded.

"Then why wasn't he called to give evidence before?" snapped the major. He was obviously anticipating another lengthy session of left-handed note taking and didn't welcome the prospect.

"Captain Garrard's evidence cannot affect the charge against the accused," the lieutenant said patiently. "He was not present at the material time." He took off his spectacles, wiped them on a handkerchief. "The time at which the accused admits striking his superior officer," he added to make matters even clearer.

"Dammit man," the major said, "if you didn't call him, how does he come to be here?"

The lieutenant adjusted his spectacles on the bridge of his nose and maintained a dignified silence. The major transferred his gaze to me. If anything, it was even more baleful than the one he'd directed at the lieutenant.

"You *are* Captain Garrard, I take it?"

I admitted it and produced my identity papers. Meadows, who had been staring impassively at a point on the opposite wall, suddenly sprang to his feet, took them from my hand and presented them to the court. It was a swift efficient action perfectly suited to an alert officer of the military police. Also, when contrasted with my own difficulty in rising, one which served to accentuate the extent of my disability. Clever, I thought. Forewarned, forearmed. The subaltern shot me a look of sympathy. Katherine wedged a crutch under one arm while I grabbed for the other. Finally erect, I faced the major. He glared back at me. Two strangers with nothing in common save our wounds. Nothing, that is, except for the fate of Sergeant Wilkins. A startling metallic clang echoed round the gynmasium as the major struck the table with the contents of his black glove.

"Say what you have to say, Captain Garrard, and make it quick. We haven't got all day." He turned to the subaltern. "I authorize you to note down the testimony. Head it—character witness. All right with you, lieutenant?"

"Perfectly acceptable, sir." He looked politely bored now, a professional permitting the amateurs to have their brief moment.

"Proceed," the major said.

I spoke slowly, allowing the subaltern plenty of time to get it all down. After a while, he gave me an encouraging nod and I speeded up a bit. Perhaps he'd studied shorthand at his school.

"With respect, Mr. President," I said, "Sergeant Wilkins is not guilty of making any statements calculated to spread alarm or undermine morale because his report was factually true and accurate. Furthermore he did not make it on his own initiative but as the result of my direct order. In view of its nature I considered it to be of the utmost urgency requiring prompt and immediate action. I was his commanding officer. He obeyed my order."

"Most praiseworthy, I'm sure," the lieutenant interrupted gently, "but the accused is charged with striking Captain Bates. A charge to which he has already pleaded guilty." He smiled at me, the maestro softening the rebuke for the tyro.

"I don't dispute that," I said, "but he did so for one reason and one reason only. Captain Bates stated that I was a liar." I paused, glanced at the court. They were all listening and the subaltern nodded to show that my last sentence had been recorded.

"I have served with Sergeant Wilkins since he was a private and I was a subaltern. In the Ypres salient."

The captain pursed his lips and for a moment his eyes clouded over. Gassed there in 1915 in all probability.

I continued quickly. "There is no need, I'm sure, to remind you that the efficiency of any fighting unit depends on loyalty—both upward and downward. If Wilkins had ever disobeyed my orders, that loyalty would have been betrayed. If I had ever lied to him when giving them, it would have been shattered beyond repair." I looked directly at the prosecuting lieutenant. "Anyone who has been in the front line knows that," I said.

It wasn't his fault that he had been nowhere near it, but the cheapest point was forgivable if it would help Wilkins. The captain coughed, covered his mouth with a stained handkerchief, disposing of phlegm. The subaltern scribbled furiously. The major pushed the black glove a few inches away from him with his left hand as though the sight of it offended him.

"The substance of this report . . ." he began, but the lieutenant cut him short.

"It's in Captain Bates's testimony, sir," he said sharply. "A vague description of some species of wild animals roaming between the lines at night."

"They were not animals," I said.

"Captain Bates," the lieutenant said quickly, "also states that he went to the trouble of checking this report with the medical officer who had attended Captain Garrard—"

"Just a minute," said the subaltern. "Sorry." He wrote rapidly, nodded to show that he was up to date.

"—in case Captain Garrard had also mentioned it to him. He had. The MO's professional opinion was that it was pure fantasy, imagination, a trick of the mind induced by the conditions in which Captain Garrard found himself. It's all there in the testimony."

"The MO's name was Selfridge," I said as they shuffled their papers. "He was an excellent surgeon, but he told me that he would have preferred being . . ." I paused, not only to allow the subaltern to catch up.

"Preferred being what?" growled the major impatiently.

"A psychiatrist," I said.

"Hearsay evidence," the lieutenant snapped. "Inadmissible."

But he was too late. The word had dropped into the stillness of the room and remained there like a softly ticking bomb. Long experience had taught the members of field general courts-martial in France to disbelieve much of the evidence presented to them. But one type stood head and shoulders above the rest as a guarantee of deliberate deception. Neither understood nor trusted, it was found safer to ignore. This was common knowledge in every barrack room, every trench between the Channel and the Swiss border.

"You want to make sure they top you, mate, get a psychiatrist to swear you're innocent."

Well, there are two sides to every coin.

"I should like," the major said slowly, "to hear from Captain Garrard's own lips exactly what he did see that night. Just as he told it to the accused . . ." He looked challengingly at the lieutenant.

". . . and to that would-be psychiatrist."

The memory will soon fade, Selfridge had said, but he'd been wrong about that, too. I remembered every detail and was able to recount them now as though they had only happened yesterday.

There were no interruptions, but once or twice I heard

Katherine's sharp intake of breath and realized that she, like the rest, apart from Wilkins himself, was hearing it in its entirety for the first time.

"It was Sergeant Wilkins who found me the next morning," I said at the end. "I owe my life to him."

There was silence while the subaltern wrote down the final words for the court record. His two fellow members sat absolutely still, their eyes seeming to look far beyond the walls of the gymnasium, back into memories they had schooled themselves to forget.

"On the Somme . . ." the major said suddenly and checked himself. "The court will adjourn," he announced in his official voice.

Wilkins was escorted out by the MPs. Katherine and I were left alone with the lieutenant. He was busily wiping his glasses, not looking at us. "Terrible," he said to the opposite wall, "I'm sorry." He spun round abruptly, his gentle face contorted with anger. "Christ, what a futile useless word! The whole bloody country will be using it soon because there's nothing else left to say. The whole world will. Sorry, they'll say." Then he too left us.

"You're shaking," Katherine said. "I've got some medicine in my bag."

"Don't need it," I said. "Only you."

She pulled her chair in front of mine, sat there gripping both my hands to hold them still.

"Every man I've nursed in that hospital," she said quietly, "they've each had their stories, things they had to speak about, get out of their systems, exorcise. But this . . ."

"We'll do it together," I said. "Exorcise it."

I didn't believe it nor, I'm sure, did she.

Meadows came back and I asked him what he thought of Wilkins's chances.

"Not much," he said. "What you told them doesn't affect the actual charge. Pity. Did your best. But there it is. Best be prepared."

Forewarned once again, I thought bitterly, forearmed.

"This war ever ends," Meadows said, "something'll have to be done about them."

I was confused. "Who?"

"Blokes you described, Garrard. Blokes you saw."

"You believed me then?"

"*I* did," Meadows said, "but I'm a trained policeman. Know the truth when I hear it."

"You don't think they will?"

"They?" Meadows asked with sudden unexpected anger. "Who's they? Lots of theys. Lesser theys have bigger theys upon their backs to bite 'em, something, something, ad bloody infinitum . . ."

He broke off, grinned at Katherine.

"Your intended's a brave man," he said. "Take care of him."

"I will," said Katherine. "What do we do now?"

"Wait. They chew it over—return—announce findings. The judges." He pronounced the final word with sour amusement. It didn't happen like that.

After an hour and a half, the subaltern came back alone. Deprived of his brief authority with pencil and paper, the shelter of the table, he looked more than ever like a gangling schoolboy, thin and vulnerable, one who had outgrown his strength.

"The major would like to see you in the old shower room, Captain Garrard," he said and blushed.

I had an alarming vision of naked bathing parties, orgies back at base, another army scandal for the troops.

"It's not in use any longer, at least for ablutions," the subaltern said hastily. "We've been allotted it for our—er—deliberations. The only place still available."

"The privations of total war," murmured Meadows.

I followed the boy out of the gymnasium and along a low, pipe-lined passage. "Probably shouldn't tell you this," he said, bending his head to avoid bumping it on the plumbing, "but we've been joined by a colonel from GHQ. Thought I'd warn you. I think he's something to do with Intelligence." He opened a door marked in fading paint, Water is Precious. Do NOT Waste. Remains of old shower fitments sprouted from the ceiling, twisted rusting roses above a floor of cracked black and white tiles. The major sat gloomily on a long wooden bench, his papers spread out beside him. The captain leaned against the outside wall next to a single open window, inhaling and exhaling noisily. From being leading players in the drama each seemed to have accepted relegation to minor roles.

Without question the new star was the tall red-tabbed officer standing in the precise center of that absurd room, dominating it and the rest of the cast with an easy air of natural authority, further enhanced by the splendor of his expensively tailored uniform, the highly polished Sam Browne, the gleaming cavalry boots. "Charles," he said, holding out his hand. "Colonel Charles. Delighted to meet you, Captain Garrard." Skin stretched tightly across prominent cheekbones, the upper part of his long angular face looked as though it had just been dry-cleaned, but his lips were surprisingly damp, full and pouting, almost like a baby's as he smiled his greeting.

"I've read the transcript of your statement," he said. "Every word." I turned toward the major but he was staring intently at the floor, clearly a man no longer provided with a speaking part.

"I was under the impression, colonel," I said, "that such statements were confidential to members of the court until they'd reached their verdict."

"Quite so, quite so," Charles said, "unless of course a question of security is involved."

I stared at him. The baby lips continued to smile but the pale grey eyes were cold, watchful. I was aware of a sudden sense of danger, a warning.

"Security, colonel?"

"That's what I said, Garrard." The lizard eyes flicked toward the major. "In this instance the presiding officer was entirely correct in referring the whole matter to me. I presume you're not questioning his judgment?" His arrogance made me ignore the warning.

"Only in so far as it might affect a man on trial for his life," I said. For a moment the mask slipped. A flash of fury in the cold eyes, a swift movement of his tongue, scything the wetness of his lips. Lizard eyes, lizard tongue. Then it was resumed.

"Fond of your sergeant, aren't you?"

"I respect him. He's a good soldier."

"Good soldiers don't attack their officers, Garrard."

He turned abruptly, marched to the captain's window, slammed it shut, fastened its worn catch, carefully placed one booted foot on the end of the major's bench. The major did not look up. The pattern of the floor tiles appeared to fascinate him, demanding his whole attention.

"However," Colonel Charles said loudly, "I'm not here because

I care about what happens to one unimportant NCO. I'm here because I care about the future of the whole damned army. About winning this war."

A drop of water plopped from a truncated pipe. The captain coughed painfully. Otherwise silence.

"Listen to me, Garrard," the colonel said, "listen carefully. Nine people in that gymnasium heard what you had to say. If any one of them repeats it, the rumor will spread like a forest fire. Within no time every man in the front line will have heard it. Wherever that may be."

"Not rumor, colonel," I said, "the truth."

He removed his foot from the bench, walked slowly across to me, stopped with his face only a few inches from mine. In those few seconds its expression had changed to a kind not normally associated with polished boots and spotless uniforms but one that I recognized only too well. Haunted, harassed, nearly but not quite afraid to hope. The look of the trenches, the front line. Colonel Charles and I in our different ways, it seemed, might after all be fighting on the same side.

"There's another truth," he said quietly. "It began at dawn last Thursday. Six thousand guns. The biggest bombardment ever known. The Germans have broken through on a forty-mile front between Lens and the Oise. They've already taken Bapaume and Peronne. Twenty miles in four days and they're still advancing. If they take Amiens . . ."

He broke off, stared unseeingly at a piece of twisted metal protruding from the wall.

"Four years of it," he said, "and all for nothing. Nothing except defeat." When he looked at me again, his smile was as sudden as it was unexpected and this time it even touched his eyes. "Sorry to sound so gloomy, Garrard, but I'm right. It's my job to know these things."

I watched him as he turned away, went back to the bench, sat down beside the major, knocking some of the papers to the floor.

"We know it's their last great effort, the last desperate throw. They know it too, every man jack of them. That's why they'll fight like tigers. And that's why we've *got* to stop them. Otherwise . . ."

He bent down, picked up the fallen papers, and the dry-cleaned face seemed suddenly crumpled with weariness, haggard. "God knows we've asked enough of our chaps already. This is the final round. The one that counts. We can't expect them to win it if they're to be continually haunted by the specter of . . . of demons appearing from the ground to violate their wounded and their dead."

"The Somme," the major said quietly, "the old battlefields." He was still staring at the tiles.

I knew then that I was not the only one who had seen them.

"I've been in touch with HQ," Colonel Charles said. "Also London. Your statement will be expunged from the records of this court-martial. It does not exist. All who heard it will be sworn to secrecy. Anyone breaking that oath will be summarily dealt with. Ruthlessly. You understand what I'm saying?"

I nodded. "Quite clearly, sir. You're suppressing evidence."

"You stupid young bugger," he said without heat. "Do you really imagine wars can be fought with clean hands?"

"I was thinking of Sergeant Wilkins, sir."

"Nor for that matter without making dubious deals, Captain Garrard." He handed the papers back to the major. "Under the circumstances," he said, "the verdict will be a reprimand and return to the line. Carry on, please."

A reprimand I knew was the lightest sentence the court could award. Virtually no punishment at all. It also occurred to me that if the situation was as desperate as the colonel had described, every possible able-bodied man was needed to stem it, especially battle-toughened sergeants, even one who had struck a superior officer.

I started to follow the major and the others out of the room, but the colonel called me back.

"You'll be going to England soon," he said. "I'm glad to tell you I've been able to fix your next appointment. The war office. Carries promotion. Reward for tribulations."

I had already requested a posting to regimental headquarters. Training duties perhaps.

"So you can keep an eye on me," I said. "Make sure I don't speak out of turn." He shook his head. "Not me, Garrard. I expect someone will, though." Lesser theys, I thought, have bigger theys. He's already provided ample proof of that.

"The nurse you have in attendance," he said. "Most attractive, if I may say so. You're planning to marry her, I understand."

How did he know that? Meadows?

"I keep my ear to the ground. Have to in my job. Contacts all over the place, you'd be surprised. Waiters in the Chat Bleu and so forth."

"What exactly is your job, sir?" I asked.

He moved quickly to the window, wrestled with the catch.

"Damn stuffy in here. Still smells of the great unwashed."

The window creaked open on rusty hinges.

"She's not strictly military, Garrard. Not bound by the Act, if you see what I mean." He looked at me earnestly. "They'll have to rely on you to see she keeps quiet," he said.

"They, sir?"

"My chaps," he said vaguely. "I'll be otherwise engaged."

He saw me looking at the medal ribbons on his chest and frowned with annoyance as though one of his darker secrets had been penetrated. "I've been on the Somme before. Know the terrain. Could be useful."

"You and Wilkins, colonel," I said.

"Anyone who can still stand and fight." He glanced at the crutches. "No offense intended."

"None taken," I said.

The door was flung open and a corporal I hadn't seen before stood there saluting.

"Transport's ready, sir."

"Go away, Melville," the colonel said, "and next time knock first."

"Sir!" barked the corporal.

"I'm not a complete bastard, you know," Colonel Charles said.

Corporal Melville grinned at me, confirming it. Then he saluted again and left us.

"One more thing, Garrard. That report of yours. I didn't actually say it was untrue. Not in so many words."

"No, sir."

"Timing," he said. "Everything's a matter of timing. Once this bloody war is over . . ." He broke off, smiled. "Sounds like the title of a soldier's song, doesn't it?"

"Something'll have to be done about them," I said, echoing Meadows. "Is that what you were going to say?"

He stared at me and for a moment I thought he was going to give me a direct answer. I was wrong.

"You asked me about my job," he said. "It *was* collecting every scrap of useful information, collating them and then giving required advice in high places. Almost invariably ignored. Such places are not noted for their appreciation of intelligence with a capital I." A tired smile flickered briefly in the lizard eyes.

"Or their possession of it with a small one. That's one of the reasons we're in such a buggers' muddle now. Only of course they won't make it sound like that. They'll find words to dress it up. Splendid empty words. They always do." He opened the door. "Thank God, I shan't have to listen to them anymore," he said. "Best of luck in the marriage stakes."

I wanted to wish him luck too, but he was already striding away down the passage, head held high in the narrow gap between the rows of pipes. It would have been pointless anyway. Where he was going you either had luck or you didn't, and mostly you didn't. He'd have known that. He'd been there before.

I didn't wish it to Wilkins either for the same reason.

"Can't go saying there ain't no justice no more, can I?"

"Certainly not."

"How d'you manage to fix it, sir?"

"I didn't."

Wilkins gave me his tell-that-to-the-Marines look.

"Who did then? The perishing prime minister?"

It was not impossible, I thought, that he'd had some remote hand in it.

"No names, no pack drill, sergeant."

"Thanks anyway. You'd never leave a bloke in the shit. Knew that from the day you came out to join us."

He looked very smart in his new uniform, quite unsuitable for the line, rather as I must have done when we first met, and that seemed half a lifetime ago.

"The esteem is mutual," I said.

"I signed that form, the one about not repeating what you said to the court."

"So did I."

"Know what it made me think of? What Major Richardson said to me once. Never forgot it. 'Soldier,' he said, 'truth is the first casualty of war.' He'd had a drop or two, mind you, but he meant it."

"A quotation," I said. "The lads'll be glad to see you back."

"Them that's left, maybe."

He took a crumpled envelope from his pocket.

"Do us one more favor, would you? My dad and me can't stand the sight of each other, but if anything happens could you see he gets this."

"I'll keep it till you can give it to him yourself."

Bromides, I thought, ready to palliate pain should yet another hoped-for truth become a casualty.

"Glad you're getting spliced. She's a lucky lady."

"I'm a lucky man."

"Tell my dad to take good care of Hilda."

"Who's Hilda?"

"My daughter."

"I didn't know you were married, Wilkins."

"I'm not," he said cheerfully, "but I am Hilda's pa. Her ma dumped her on our doorstep when she was six months old. She's nearly two now. I knew I shouldn't have taken that home leave. More peaceful to keep fighting." Whistles shrilled, orders were shouted. The troop train was ready to leave. Wilkins saluted.

"Sod 'em all," he said. "Look after yourself, sir."

"You too, sergeant," I called after him.

It seemed a poor way to say good-bye to a man for whom, I suddenly realized as he marched away, I felt something very much akin to love.

I watched an elderly and harassed MP, his arms flailing wildly as he tried to direct soldiers to the right compartments.

"Sod you, for starters," I heard Wilkins tell him cheerfully.

Then he was gone.

CHAPTER 7

They were all going, every man who could be spared, moving up to the westward bulging line, pieces of human cement to strengthen the wall against the German advance. Not only the British from the Etaples area, weary fatalistic French in the central sector, newly arrived American divisions streaming north from their training grounds around Chaumont to hold the St. Mihiel salient.

Meadows went. "Know how to deal with 'em," he said when he came to say good-bye to Katherine and myself. "Tell 'em I'm a redcap. Scare 'em back to hell."

"Who?" Katherine asked.

Meadows looked at me. "Your future husband knows," he said. "He's seen 'em. Blokes crawling out of craters." He smiled as he spoke, but it wasn't a joke. Roy Meadows was as usual forewarned and forearmed, even against devils.

Passchendaele was given up, then the woods through which we had fought, even the ridge at Messines. The German army was at the gates of Ypres once again. Our bitter costly advance of six months earlier might never have been. Nothing to show for it but the unnumbered unnecessary dead, the cripples like myself, men who could no longer stand and fight. Not that I wished to from any sense of duty or patriotic fervor. By now such phrases belonged only to the debased coinage of John Bull journalism. I simply wanted to be with the only men I still trusted, those I had learned to respect, my friends.

The enemy attack continued across the old battlefields of the Somme. Douai fell, Cambrai. They came dangerously close to Amiens, and on the Marne, Paris itself was within less than forty miles.

But they found the words just as Colonel Charles had said they would. On April 12th, Field Marshal Haig issued his Order of the Day, read out to every soldier in the line, repeated in newspapers throughout Britain.

> There is no other course open to us but to fight it out. Every position must be held to the last man. There must be no retirement. With our backs to the wall and believing in the justice of our cause, each one must fight on to the end . . .

Splendid empty words, the colonel had prophesied, and in the sense that Haig and his like had been preaching much the same message for nearly four years, he was undoubtedly right. Sergeant Wilkins certainly thought so. A few days later Katherine received a letter stamped with the military censor's seal of approval. It was addressed to Sister Poole and Friend, The Hospital, Le Touquet, and apart from those in brackets, was devoid of any marks of punctuation.

> Bless all clever kitchen staff Thank operating wizards Having all tonics without any lasting lavatory (?) troubles Hope every one of nurses eating apples to get headstrong quacks (?) held at bay Look out or Doctor youknowwho hopes attack (!)

The nursing staff was well accustomed to cryptic communications from former patients and usually the correspondent was immediately remembered, sometimes with affection, occasionally with relief at his departure. This one defied identification. Mystified, Katherine showed it to me. I deciphered the almost illegible signature and the rest was easy.

"Don't never pay no heed to them censors," I remembered him saying. "Just read the first letter of each word and it's a doddle. Takes time, but what else have we got in between trying to be sodding heroes?"

I did as instructed.

Backs to what wall? The one at GHQ? Ha bloody ha!

GHQ was in a château at Montreuil and I've no doubt that Wilkins expressed the thoughts of the vast majority of those actually doing the fighting. Other very essential weapons besides guns were necessary to preserve life in the trenches, notably a sense of humor and an undefeated spirit.

Next day I sailed from Boulogne in an almost empty troopship immediately after it had landed yet another batch of reinforcements in France. I stood with Katherine on the dockside watching them disembark. Some could hardly have left their preparatory schools when it all began, others were veterans in their early twenties returning from foreshortened furloughs, a few, much older, looking surprised and worried as though uncomfortably aware that they had reached the wrong destination. But all had one thing in common. They could still stand and fight.

Katherine was due for two months' leave in the autumn, and I told her that the first thing we must do when she arrived in England was to get married.

"You have an entirely Victorian sense of priorities," she said and laughed as she kissed me.

"You mean I should ask your father's permission first?"

"I mean that I'm tired of watching you lying in a bed without being in it with you," she said.

"Well spoken, madam," said a voice from among the small group of passengers passing us on their way to the ship. I looked round but could see no one that I recognized.

"I love you, you fool," Katherine said, "and I'm too impatient to wait for Mother Church to bless us before proving it. I should get to London on September twenty-fifth. A suite at the Ritz looking over Piccadilly and with a large double bed would be rather nice at least for one night, don't you think?"

When I eventually reported for duty at the war office I was given a small room containing two telephones. One was red, only to be employed for matters of extreme importance. I much enjoyed using it for the first time in order to arrange our booking at the Ritz.

* * *

The voice on the dockside, it transpired, had belonged to an old acquaintance and had I been able to see his black-gloved hand then, I'd have identified him immediately.

"Askew," he said as he joined me on the gently rolling deck in mid-channel. "Major Askew. Good to see the old white cliffs again, isn't it? Good to see you too, Garrard."

I remembered him seated behind the table in the Etaples gymnasium, tilting a little toward his left as he wrote painstakingly with his one good hand. The name, which I'd never heard before, seemed to suit him. He was tilted again now against the motion of the ship.

"Glad to have this opportunity for a chat," he said. "Always wanted to tell you that I should never have presided at that damn court-martial."

I asked him why, although I was fairly certain I already knew the answer.

"Those creatures you described," he said, "those men. I'd seen the same myself. On the Somme near Ginchy, back in '16."

He lifted his false right hand, regarded it with distaste. Whatever was inside the black glove remained rigid and steady in the wind from the bows. "The night I lost this," he said, and looked away toward the English coast, "I thought I was a goner out there in No Man's Land. That's when I saw them."

He was silent for a full minute. I knew what he was remembering and made no attempt to prompt him.

"They weren't only English and French, Garrard. Germans as well. I speak their language, you know. I'm an interpreter."

A small note of pride had crept into his voice. Understanding the tongue of the enemy was considered a valuable adjunct to the general business of killing him.

"Yes," I said. "I heard one speak German, too."

He gripped the rail tightly with his left hand, swung round to face me, his eyes haunted.

"Soldiers from all the warring armies living together down there beneath the earth in some sort of unimaginable hell. In some sort of demented . . ." He paused, unable to find the right word.

"Peace?" I suggested.

The black glove swung upward, and for a moment I thought he was going to smash it into my face.

"Cowards," he muttered angrily. "Deserters."

Then he got control of himself again.

"I made my report," he said, "just as your sergeant did. Only not to some regimental officer. To divisional HQ. I was told to keep my mouth shut. Ordered to forget it. From a great height and in no uncertain terms." He stared down at the sparkling bow wave. "So I knew what was bound to happen, d'you see? That Colonel Charles must call the whole thing off—make his deal."

"That's why you referred it to him?"

Major Askew nodded. "I had to. Too important for me to handle alone. Too important even for him. He spoke direct to the DMI's office."

"Who?"

"Director of Military Intelligence. No doubt they consulted higher authority. Downing Street perhaps, who knows?"

Lesser theys have bigger theys, I thought, and so ad infinitum.

"Those men," I said, "those deserters or whatever they are— d'you think they're still there?"

He stared back toward the French coast, a dark smudge on the horizon. It looked peaceful but we could still hear the rumble of the guns.

"More now than before, I shouldn't wonder." He laughed, a bitter sound. "Each one must fight on to the end. Well, they'll fight in their own way when it comes to it. Not yet. When it's all over. When something has to be done about them."

"What?" I said.

"Don't ask me, Garrard. Ask them when you get to the war house. Not that they'll tell you, of course. Just say they'd prefer you not to rock the boat until it's ready to put to sea. They like damn silly metaphors, talking in riddles. Suits their image."

I could make out the breakwater of Dover harbor now, a snaking black line sprouting from the base of the white wall above it.

"Who exactly d'you mean, Askew?"

He lifted the black glove, pointed it toward the shore.

"Our future masters. The keepers of secrets. Particularly awkward ones like ours. I take it we *are* both destined for the same fate? Some trumped-up, totally unnecessary job where they can keep an eye on us, see we don't get out of line. Time to collect our gear now, I think." He turned away from the rail, moved toward companionway leading down to the main deck.

"The DMI's office?" I asked.

He stopped at the head of the stairs, grinned back at me.

"Part of it. Military Operations, section five. I met a few of them when I was qualifying as an interpreter. Most inquisitive lot. Love asking questions, hate giving answers. Wanted to make sure I wasn't a German spy or something." The ship heeled suddenly as it turned into the swept channel outside the harbor entrance, and he grabbed at the stair rail with his good hand to steady himself.

"They're called MO5 for short," he said.

He was wrong about that.

"Our title was changed eighteen months ago," Brigadier Henry Messiter said as he showed me into my small room with the two telephones. "We're no longer known as MO5. We are now MI5. Sounds a touch more incisive, wouldn't you say? Keener."

He was smiling as he spoke. The smile was such an integral part of his round benevolent face that one felt he must have been born with the basic prototype already in place, allowing the years to add a variety of improved models designed to meet changing moods or situations. This one was clearly the welcome model. He looked like a kindly schoolmaster, reassuringly unathletic, comfortably overweight, the sort beloved and trusted by small boys who would instinctively feel that at heart he was still one of them, understanding their problems, sharing their ambitions, gentle with their misdemeanors. He wore thick pebble glasses which hid the expression in his eyes.

"I hope you'll be comfortable in here, Major Garrard," he said and pointed proudly at the chair in front of the desk. "I ordered that specially for you. It's mounted on little wheels. Saves wear and tear on the old legs."

His voice was quiet yet crisp, his phrasing typical of an English public school education. But there was something unusual about the accent, a sort of pleasing lift on the final words of each sentence.

"Like myself," he said, "it's made in America. My dear mother is a rich but highly intelligent lady from New York, my esteemed father a comparatively impecunious but equally brainy don at Oxford. A happy progeniture, wouldn't you say? Affords me a useful sense of balance. Like that chair. Do try it, won't you?"

I did so, swooping effortlessly from one end of the desk to the other while he looked on with proprietorial approval.

"Splendid," he said. "I must request another from a friend of mine on General Pershing's staff. A good man, Pershing. His Americans have brought us a measure of comfort on the home front besides stirring victories in the field."

"Belleau Wood," I said to show him that I was keeping abreast of the situation, "and Château-Thierry."

"Precisely, dear boy. And when they attack in the St. Mihiel salient it will assuredly be, as my dear mother would say, one hell of a home run." He smiled. The modest model.

"Forgive my New World pride but blood will out. Now, as to *your* actual duties . . ."

He did his best to make them sound important and enjoyable, but they were, as Askew had forecast, manufactured for the occasion, time-consuming but clearly superfluous. They consisted of collating and filing a long list of people suspected, for one reason or another, of being sympathetic to the German cause. The major was doing much the same sort of thing on the floor below except that his list was composed of those Germans who might qualify as trustworthy in some as yet unspecified type of post-war collaboration. Later we discovered that every name mentioned on either list belonged to someone who had been dead for several years. There was no shortage of such inventories in the War Office.

I performed my chores during the day while the major carried out his at night. In this way, the brigadier explained, one of us would always be available to deal wth important telephone calls. I rarely received any, important or otherwise.

"All vital to the greater struggle," Messiter concluded. "They also serve who only sit and collate."

His smile was still welcoming, his eyes still hidden.

As he was about to leave, a fresh thought seemed to occur to him.

"I quite forgot to enquire about your digs," he said apologetically. "I trust you find them congenial."

They were in a small apartment off Whitehall, two bedrooms, a sitting room, bathroom, and kitchen, palatial compared with anything I'd been accustomed to in the last few years. I shared it with Major Askew, but we had little opportunity for conversation since whenever one of us returned from our duties the other was always on the point of leaving to begin his. I developed an unhealthy curiosity as to what he did with his false hand when he had a bath, but was never able to satisfy it. The bathroom was invariably bereft of everything except his shaving gear and a bar of Lifebuoy soap, meticulously clean. He was a tidy man and, since his revelations on the boat, an uncommunicative one. I learned virtually nothing of his private life except that his first name was Edward and that he had an unmarried sister living in Hitchin with whom he spent an occasional weekend. However, I liked him, and when later I asked him to be the best man at my wedding, he accepted with alacrity.

"I'd thought of looking for somewhere a bit cheaper," I said to the brigadier, "in Kensington perhaps." This wasn't true but I was anxious to discover whether the major had exaggerated their determination to keep us under constant supervision.

"Don't give it another thought," the brigadier said heartily. "Your rent is paid by a grateful HMG. We take pride in looking after our people. Like to feel they're close at hand if needed. Any problems, come straight to me. You're one of the family now."

The smile didn't flicker as he raised a hand in farewell before closing the door. I swirled the chair around, picked up the red telephone, and asked for the number of the Ritz Hotel. They would have learned of my intended truancy eventually anyway, so why make them wait? It was a small gesture of defiance, of independence, and as I've said, I enjoyed making it.

The brigadier sent me a note a week or so later. "Delighted to hear you've chosen to welcome your fiancée at the best hotel in London. We can hardly expect HMG to foot the bill for the suite, but I've taken the liberty of arranging champagne on the house or rather the department. Just make yourselves known to the head waiter."

I could imagine his smile as he composed it. The satisfied model. Further evidence that he looked after his boys, saw to it that they were kept out of mischief, and I had to admit, he did it with considerable style.

In the end I had to ask his permission to delay my night of freedom at the Ritz. Katherine was arriving four days later than expected. He showed no surprise, agreed at once. In all probability, one of his untitled files contained up-to-date information on everyone returning from France, just as others held more arcane secrets dealing with long-range weather reports relative to the advisability of when and where to use poison gas or the possibility of tanks getting bogged down in mud, the position and state of morale of each Allied regiment if not platoon, and for all I knew, detailed astrological forecasts as to General Ludendorff's health and future prospects.

"Leave it to me, Garrard. I've always found the management most cooperative. Arrangements regarding champagne remain as before, of course."

By then, while Major Askew and I had been laboring on our endless lists, the Germans had been halted at the Marne and the Allies had begun to counterattack in every sector. The Americans were advancing in the south, the British, Australian, New Zealand, and French divisions fighting once more across old battlefields of the Somme. By the beginning of September, Bapaume, Peronne and St. Quentin were in our hands. Toward its end, when General Plumer's Second Army launched their final drive to break out of the blood-soaked Ypres salient, only God and possibly Brigadier Messiter knew with any accuracy what the toll in lives had been, and neither revealed his secrets.

Katherine had more than a vague idea though. She had watched the wounded being brought in, seen their torn bodies, listened to their voices crying out in the nights when drugged sleep failed to subdue the nightmares of memory. Still in her nurse's uniform, her eyes dark with shadows, she told me of these things as we drove from the station, and I remained silent, letting her talk, knowing that she had to lay the ghosts before she could speak of anything else.

"Proper turnaround, ain't it guv?" said the elderly taxicab driver as we stopped outside the Ritz. "The soldier greeting the lady back from the horrors of war. Whatever shall we see next?"

"Women cab drivers, with a bit of luck," Katherine told him and suddenly laughed, throwing her arms around me and kissing me full on the lips in the middle of the crowded Piccadilly pavement.

Bell boys materialized, lifted out her cases. Each might have been a fully paid-up member of the brigadier's information gathering corps, but I didn't care. I cared for nothing except that the shadows had gone from Katherine's eyes, that we were truly together once more.

The hoarse voice of a newspaper seller echoed through the

arcade. "Allies advance in Flanders." Even that meant nothing. It belonged to another world. Ours was here and just beginning.

We finished a bottle of the brigadier's champagne, toasting each other and the future, and after dinner went into the other room. A second bottle stood in a silver ice bucket beside the big double bed. Katherine surveyed them both with delighted approval.

"Just as I imagined it," she said and then, more quietly, her voice not quite steady. "I've never drunk champagne in bed before. Only the very rich do that, don't they?"

"We're the richest in the world tonight," I said. "Shall we try it?"

"With joy," Katherine said.

We drank none of it. There are far greater marvels than mere champagne, infinitely greater pleasures. We found and shared them together, a magic voyage of exploration, each new discovery more wondrous than the last, an unbelievable fulfillment, completeness, joy.

Light was filtering through a chink in the curtains before we fell asleep, and I remember Katherine's drowsy, contented whisper as she closed her eyes.

"Never mind," she said. "We'll have the champagne for breakfast."

I remember too the warmth of her body close against mine as though we were still joined and now could never be separated.

But sleep did separate us, nightmare rather. I was alone again in the ruined desolation of No Man's Land, and the black creatures were crawling toward me, and I could not move. I heard their howling, the dreadful sucking sound of the mud as their leader forced himself closer and closer and then the mocking inhuman laughter as its claws arched down. I tried to close my eyes to escape the terror, but I could still see its black cowled face looming always closer to mine, the eyes red-rimmed, expressionless, dead. The face of Sergeant Wilkins.

Sixty feet beneath the ravaged surface of the Stroombeek Valley, the one the others called the Priest bent almost double as he moved through a labyrinth of interlinking lanes carved out of the deep clay. He was followed, as always, by the boy the others had christened the Acolyte.

This boy, who was still very young, had lied about his age in order to be able to fight for his country, and the Priest, who felt a responsibility for all in his parish, felt a special personal one for the Acolyte because he had found him lost and wandering and led him to where he was now, to safety. All of them, even the morose and silent ones who never spoke to anyone else, spoke to him. They liked to do so, perhaps because his youth reminded them that they too were once young. For them he represented a talisman, a symbol of some sort of hope.

The Acolyte carried a candle. He had no need of it himself for he was blind. He carried it to light the way of the Priest.

Occasionally, in one of the few more open spaces where the ceilings were a little higher, the Priest would pause and stand almost upright, his lips moving silently as his eyes swept over the groups of men huddled together on the damp earth. He was counting his flock. One hundred and forty, he said to himself as he turned to go back to his own quarters, the small innermost cavern he shared with Shaw, the Marksman, and the Shouter.

Last time he had done this there had been a hundred and fifty-three; once there had been more than two hundred. He had never performed a service of interment because the dead were already buried along with the living. But there should be prayers for them, he thought, prayers for the dead. As always he was prepared, holding in one hand a rusting tin cup, in the other a lump of stale rotting bread.

"Holy Communion?" he asked as he moved through his flock, and repeated the question in several tongues.

No one answered it.

The Priest was the fourth of the leaders.

CHAPTER 8

I woke trembling with Katherine holding me close, one hand gently wiping the icy sweat from my forehead. She had witnessed enough soldiers' nightmares to know that words alone were unable to dispel them. Only the reassurance of human contact could do that, a patient silent guidance back from the dark shadows into the comforting light of reality.

Later, after I'd been able to describe the horror of the dream to her, she said, "I didn't tell you this before because I hated to remind you of what had happened, but they asked me to make a written report if any of the wounded at Le Touquet claimed to have seen what you saw."

"They?" I asked, already knowing the answer.

"An intelligence officer from Etaples. I think he was attached to GHQ. He used to send a courier over once a fortnight."

"To you personally? No one else?"

She nodded.

And then, I thought, he'd pass the information on to the brigadier. Lesser theys to greater theys, carefully keeping it in the family, and Katherine was one of them because she'd heard my statement at the court-martial. Colonel Charles would have told them that.

Neither of us felt like drinking champagne for breakfast and I asked Katherine to give it to her parents, a suitable present from her fiancé.

It was September 29th, the day the ridge of Passchendaele was conquered at last. A week later I learned that George Wilkins had been killed in that final brave assault.

I waited till the brief telegram of regrets had been sent to his father from the War Office and on the next Sunday morning took the train to Croydon and gave him his son's letter. He worked as caretaker of a big ugly boarding house and lived in a large cheerless room on the ground floor, divided in half by a thin plasterboard wall with a door at its center. The place was unheated, and he kept shivering in spite of two stained cardigans draped around his bony shoulders. Hilda was presumably on the other side of the partition.

He held the envelope in his hands, peered at it through ancient spectacles, but did not open it.

"Like a cup of tea?" he said.

It wasn't yet midday, but I could hardly refuse, and he boiled a kettle on a gas ring beside the unlit fire.

"George took after my missus. Him and me never really hit it off."

"He was a fine soldier," I said, "a valued friend."

The old man removed the spectacles and blinked at me, a sort of challenge.

"You're going to tell me I ought to be proud of him, are you?"

"I'm sure you are," I said.

"Why? On account of he's dead?"

"Because he lived bravely," I said, "because he always thought of others' safety before his own, because—"

"Cannon fodder," he interrupted. "No more, no less, meat for the slaughterhouse." He chuckled, a dry humorless rattle, false teeth clacking. "Said as much himself."

I felt a deep hopeless anger and knew I had to suppress it.

"He saved my life," I said.

Wilkins senior got slowly to his feet, took a colored tin from the mantelpiece. It was decorated with the faces of King George and Queen Mary, wearing crowns.

"Did he? Where was that then?"

"Passchendaele," I told him, "very near to Passchendaele."

For the first time he showed a real spark of interest.

"I've heard of that," he said. "They took it at the end of what they call the third battle of Ypres, that right?"

I nodded and he continued with enthusiasm.

"It started when they blew up the Messines Ridge. Heard the explosion here in Croydon, I did. Woke me up. I thought it was thunder but a jar of my baccy fell off the table. Thunder wouldn't have done that. Soon after three in the morning it was. I'll always remember, June the seventh last year, 1917." He glared at me, proud of his powers of recall, daring me to contradict them. "And then they let the bloody Germans turf them out again. Senseless. What's the point of it all? What *is* the bloody point, I ask you."

He lifted the lid from the tin, held it out in my direction. "You take sugar?"

Such luxuries were still rationed. I shook my head.

"We've retaken it now," I said.

"Backwards and forwards," he muttered. "Forwards and backwards. Senseless, bloody senseless."

I decided not to tell him that Passchendaele was where his son had died. He would be sent the full official details along with the full official regrets in due course anyway. We drank our tea in silence while he read the letter slowly and with difficulty, holding it close to his spectacles.

"Know what he says here?" he asked, putting down his empty cup. " 'Look after my Hilda and stop grumbling, Dad. Things'll get better if I'm not there to drive you barmy.' "

A child wailed suddenly from the other side of the partition.

"Always complaining," the old man said, "just like her father. Bet the little brute's wet herself."

He pulled open the door, disappeared, slamming it behind him. Two minutes later he was back holding Hilda in his arms.

"I was right. She was sopping."

I peered at the child. Straggling black hair, thin cheeks puckered in fury, a purple birthmark discoloring the left one. But I thought I could detect a slight resemblance to Wilkins in one of his more violent officer-baiting moods.

"Pretty little thing," I said.

"Do us a favor," Wilkins's father said. "Don't feed us no more lies."

I explained that I couldn't stay long because there was only one train back to London that day. He nodded without interest, crumpled the letter into a tight ball between his hands, his eyes staring blankly at the sugar tin.

"I got sent to day school up the East End when I was a kid. There was a padre used to come in Fridays. No matter who you are, he'd tell us, don't you ever forget that each one of you is precious in the sight of God. Every human life is a thing of wonder, a thing of dignity."

He threw the screwed-up paper into the fireplace.

"Only doing his duty, I suppose," he said. "Stupid sod."

I didn't know whether he was referring to the padre, his son, or his grandchild. It didn't seem to matter.

I looked back at the house from the other side of the road after saying good-bye. He had retrieved the letter, smoothed out its crumpled pages, was standing with them in his hands, his shoulders bent as though under some load too heavy for him to bear. He'd turned on a gas lamp to help him see the words more clearly and in its flickering light I could see the tears glistening on his cheeks. The other half of the room was in darkness, but I could hear the sound of Hilda's wailing.

I walked to the station, and the sound of the engine raising steam seemed to echo the name—Passchendaele . . . Passchendaele— and when the carriage jerked forward, its wheels continued to drum the same word against the track, iron-hard now, as pitilessly repetitive as the deaths of those who had given their lives to gain that place of the already dead, that dread talisman of victory.

The train slowed through the London suburbs, stopped altogether for a few minutes beside a row of display hoardings, a break in the monotonous succession of small grey houses, the grubby rubbish-strewn strips which served them as gardens. It began to rain. Two men were pasting over a flaking poster of Lloyd George imploring all loyal citizens to buy war bonds, covering it with a fresh one which proclaimed in tall red, white and blue letters that Britain must be Ready and Proud to Welcome Home Her Heroes, Eager to Give Them Jobs Worthy of Their Courage and Fortitude. The face of one man was furrowed with two deep scars, and the old khaki forage cap he wore was tilted forward but not far enough to hide a third running down from the center of his skull.

His companion held a tin of paste wedged firmly between his chest and the upper part of his left arm. There was no lower part. Two of the heroes it seemed were already enjoying their nation's gratitude, the benevolence of eager employers. The rain beat down on them but they took no notice. They were used to rain.

The dignity of human life, I thought, a thing precious in the eyes of God.

Next day I wrote to Wilkins's father giving him my address and asking him not to hesitate to let me know if he needed financial assistance regarding Hilda's upbringing and welfare. He never did hesitate, and he must have told her where the money came from because years later, long after he'd died, she appeared on my doorstep and asked if I required a housekeeper.

CHAPTER 9

Katherine and I were married on the first day of November, 1918, at the beautiful church of Minster, deep in the Valency valley where she had walked as a child. Her father, a tall tranquil man in a tweed suit, which bulged with half-concealed thermometers and stethoscopes, was called away before the service began to attend a premature birth in Tintagel.

"They tend to arrive early in these parts," he said. "Can't wait to get into our world. Very strange when you consider the state it's in."

He beckoned me to follow him outside. The churchyard sloped steeply down from the small narrow road above and even now was full of flowers.

"Nevertheless," he said, "I remain an optimist. A doctor must. Hobson's choice. So I sincerely hope you and my daughter will have children who'll be able to live their lives in peace. That is the only possible vindication for any generation having descended into war."

He smiled briefly as we shook hands, an oddly formal gesture but also one which somehow both gave and received understanding, in its way a blessing mutually bestowed.

The remainder of the small congregation stayed the full course of the ceremony. Katherine's mother in a floral dress, broad-brimmed hat and white kid gloves, the whole ensemble reminiscent of Edwardian garden fêtes, a few family friends, Major Askew in the role of best man, a beaming young subaltern whom the brigadier had insisted should drive us to Cornwall and who was presumably still present to ensure that neither of us revealed any of England's official secrets while observing the rituals of her official church. The vicar wished us luck, spoke with enthusiasm of new beginnings, not only for ourselves but the whole world, and perhaps for the first time in four years the good man really believed in what he was saying. The morning papers had carried news of Ludendorff's dismissal, rumors of mutiny in the German fleet. The scent of victory was in the air.

We stayed the weekend with Katherine's parents and on the first evening of our married life her mother insisted on drinking a toast to our future progeny.

"Let's hope," she said, blushing slightly, "that the first will be a Cancerian. Such a nice sign."

Dr. Poole smiled at his daughter, winked at me.

"Or possibly even a Gemini," he said, "a far more enterprising one. I approve of Geminis."

I realized then that he knew of our premarital night at the Ritz and approved of that, too.

The subaltern drove us back to London on the Monday, told us that arrangements had already been made for Major Askew to move into rooms next door. The apartment off Whitehall would be Katherine's and my first home together. She thought this remarkably generous of my employers until I reminded her that two could be watched as cheaply as one. The subaltern treated this as a huge joke, laughing heartily and pretending to lose control of the steering.

But the watching, the brigadier's need for secrecy, exaggerated or not, was almost over. Four days later he invited himself to dinner.

"I trust you'll forgive the intrusion," he said as I opened the door, "but it's been a somewhat *mouvementé* day and I felt the need to relax among friends." He wore mufti, carried a bulky briefcase.

"I didn't realize you knew my wife," I said.

He raised Katherine's hand to his lips.

"Not directly, but I've had the pleasure of reading her reports. May I say it is nothing to that of meeting her in person."

He took a bottle of champagne from his case.

"To encourage bon appétit, dear lady."

He sat down in our one armchair, and I suddenly saw how tired he was. Even the smile seemed to require an effort.

"I've spent a large part of the last twenty-four hours talking in French," he said. "Almost as long speaking German. I am reputedly trilingual, but even so it is apt to be a trifle wearing."

I opened the champagne, poured three glasses. The brigadier drained his and accepted another before he spoke again.

"I won't beat about the bush, Garrard. You're no fool and you must have known for a long time that your job has been no more than a means of keeping you occupied until I was able to offer you a more useful one."

It might have been his champagne but it was, after all, my apartment, and I felt no obligation to allow him to get away with only a half-truth.

"Also as a means of keeping me under observation," I said.

His expression didn't alter.

"Of course. You and your wife, among others, are in possession of facts which, had they become generally known, might have led to a serious disintegration of morale. To wholesale mutiny even."

Since he was about to play his ace, I took a further perverse pleasure in trumping it.

"You mean that other soldiers might have decided they'd had enough of fighting over the same old ground and decided to join their comrades underneath it."

He put down his glass, stared at it. No hint of a smile touched his lips. Without one, his face looked unnaturally naked, like that of a man who has unexpectedly shaved off a well-known beard.

"Precisely," he said, "although I wouldn't dignify them with the name of comrades. Deserters, Garrard, cowards. Creatures was your original description, I believe. Animals."

He glanced at Katherine as though seeking confirmation.

"They're still men," she said with surprising firmness, "men driven out of their minds by others already mad. By the destruction of the spirit."

He took a cigarette from a gunmetal case, lit it. I'd never seen him smoke before.

"Possibly, dear lady, but not all are mentally deranged. Any form of society, clandestine or otherwise, must have its leaders, its thinkers, its lawmakers. Without them it would disintegrate, cease to exist."

"Are you sure these still do?" I asked.

"Quite sure. In large numbers. Hundreds, perhaps more.

Both Allied and German. At my direction Colonel Charles has been conducting certain experiments—"

He stopped speaking abruptly as though he had already said more than he intended, stubbed his unfinished cigarette into an ashtray, ground it to pulp.

"They must be rooted out," he said, "each and every one of them. Literally rooted out. Arrested as deserters. Handed over to their own military authorities. Discreet trials. Punishment without publicity."

"For the sick ones too?" Katherine asked, "the mentally deranged?"

"There are institutions," the brigadier said vaguely. "That will be for their individual courts-martial to decide."

He took another cigarette, tapped it on his case.

"Such operations must remain secret for obvious reasons," he said. "No one on either side who has tried to fight this war with some degree of honor would wish to draw attention to its least honorable and most shameful aspect."

Katherine poured the last of the champagne into his glass.

"Nor to the fact that a lot of so-called enemies refused to go on killing each other and decided that their only real enemy was the war itself," she said.

Messiter stared at her quizzically.

"If that is intended as a question, dear lady, I'm afraid that being neither a clever politician nor Almighty God I am in no position to provide an answer. I shall therefore ignore it."

He went on to tell me that while he would remain in overall charge of the proposed project at the War Office, I would be serving in the field as second in command to Colonel Charles. Further details regarding personnel and locations would be given to me when the colonel himself returned to England. In the meanwhile I was to speak of it to no one.

"Anthony Charles requested your appointment personally," he said. "It carries promotion to the acting rank of lieutenant colonel."

He didn't inquire as to whether or not I was willing to accept it. He was no longer interested in asking questions, only in giving orders.

"I don't imagine they'll exactly cooperate in being rooted out," I said.

"You know the rules for deserters attempting to resist arrest as well as I do, Garrard."

I did. You warned them once, and if they ignored it, you shot them. Men on the run had usually thrown away their arms and moved singly, at most in small groups. A hundred or more carrying weapons and concealed in underground redoubts, however primitive, were a very different matter. Especially if, having already lost their minds, they had nothing more to lose. I said as much.

The brigadier levered himself up from his chair, moved to the window, stood with his back to us breathing in the night air. His shoulders sagged a little.

"If normal methods prove inadequate," he said, "others will be provided. It's all been foreseen. *Prévu*, as the French say."

He turned but did not look at us, stared instead at his unlit cigarette.

"Gas," he said, "poison gas."

There was silence in the room. I picked up the matches, lit his cigarette.

"The Germans have been consulted," he said calmly. "They are in full agreement."

He drew deeply on his cigarette, sighed.

"You appear surprised that I should have been in touch with the enemy," he said, "but I assure you that I am not the only one. I told you it had been a full day. At seven o'clock this morning an official delegation from their supreme command arrived by train in the forest of Compiègne. They asked Marshal Foch for the conditions under which the Allies were prepared to grant them an armistice. Such conditions do exist in words but not in actuality. The German surrender, to all intents and purposes, will be unconditional. That is what Foch told them."

Far away on the river a tug hooted. Katherine gripped my hand very tightly, her voice scarcely more than a whisper.

"Did they accept that?"

"They asked for time," the brigadier said. "They were granted three days. Until eleven A.M. next Monday. November eleventh."

He fumbled at the catch of his briefcase, not looking at us.

"Till then the fighting continues," he said heavily. "Our decision, I regret to say."

Better than I, probably better than anyone, he knew how

many more would be slaughtered in the space of those three days. He lifted up a second bottle of champagne.

"In the interim," he said, "let us ask God's forgiveness for our presumption in drinking this by way of premature celebration and at the same time pray that November eleventh will indeed bring peace to us all."

He released the wire on the cork and it shot out like a bullet, smashing into the ceiling.

"Damage to government property," he said, "most reprehensible," and allowed the bubbling liquid to overflow into my glass.

He telephoned for his car as soon as we had eaten, thanked Katherine for the dinner and kissed her hand once more, looking ironically at me as he did so.

"There is one question you have not asked me, Garrard, and I must say I'm surprised at the omission."

I could think of many but I wanted to be rid of him, to be alone with Katherine.

"What's that, sir?"

"My reason for giving you this information here instead of in my office. The answer is simple. I wanted your wife to hear it too. I hope that when the time comes she will also agree to play her part. Not, of course, in the front line, as it were. In that same place where she has already rendered such valuable service. Le Touquet. One must be prepared for all eventualities, the possibility of casualties requiring hospitalization. If so, they must be attended by someone already privy to their work. Men under stress, wounded men, are apt to talk a great deal about their experiences."

He looked gravely at Katherine.

"I need hardly remind you of that."

"Hardly," she said dryly.

"There will be qualified doctors present. Should they consider it necessary, any patients will be transferred directly to your care, Mrs. Garrard. You will nurse them. Only you. No one else. I very much hope that you will agree."

"I'll think about it," Katherine said before I could protest.

"Please do," Messiter said. "I cannot imagine anyone else who would be able to fulfill the task with more expertise and resourcefulness."

I opened the front door for him.

"Or with more discretion," he added.

Watching from the window I fancied for a moment that I recognized the driver of his car but then dismissed the thought as being impossible. They drove away, turned into the darkness of Whitehall.

The telephone woke me at four A.M.

"A change in plans," said the brigadier's voice. "You will be flown to an airfield near Calais at ten o'clock this morning. I've laid on transport to meet you and take you to a rendezvous with Colonel Charles. He has now rejoined his cavalry regiment at an advanced position in Belgium and he wants to talk to you before he returns to England."

Thus it was, in the closing moments of a war in which the cavalry had played only a minor and increasingly anachronistic part, that I found myself on the morning of November 11th at Colonel Charles's headquarters just north of Maubeuge on the river Sambre.

Outside his simple campaign tent, a squadron of his dragoons waited with their horses, hidden in a copse of trees whose leafy branches remained intact, untouched by gunfire. The colonel's uniform was still immaculately creased, spotless, the high-cheekboned face still wearing its dry-cleaned look. He might have come straight from his tailors on the way to his club. We were less than a mile from the agreed German armistice lines on the other side of a bend in the river. He greeted me warmly, recalled our last meeting, regretted the necessity of having had me transferred to the War Office, hoped I hadn't been too bored there.

"Each time you send for me," I said, "I seem to end up getting promotion."

He smiled. "I'm afraid my detective work for Henry Messiter took rather longer than either of us anticipated. Not surprising, though, when you remember that the quarry hasn't merely gone to ground but actually disappeared under it. However, the first stage is now completed and at last, thank God, I'm back where I belong."

Not on his way to the club, I thought, already there. The ancient and exclusive Club of the Cavalry.

"The first stage?"

"Find them, then let us proceed to root them out," he said in a spirited imitation of the brigadier. "A characteristically colorful instruction, but somewhat lacking in precise detail. One could hardly be expected to go rooting through half of western Europe. To put up foxes one must first locate their principal earths. That's what I've been doing. That was the first stage."

He took a thin silver flask and two silver cups from a leather holder, poured brandy for each of us.

"Men living underground," he said, "must not only be able to breathe but also able to eat. Field rations ripped in the darkness of the night from the dead and dying don't exactly provide an abundant fare. So I decided to supplement it. Arranged for bundles of food and drink to be left in the various areas where such nocturnal raids had been reported. Always close to open shell craters, the deeper ravines, anything which might lead on down to some sort of air duct. For a long time and in many different locations they remained untouched. Then one morning one of them had disappeared. We'd been watching, but we hadn't seen anyone grab it. That was our mistake. I waited a few days then planted another a mile or so away. And that's when they made theirs."

"You saw them take it?"

He shook his head. "It was still there at daylight with a message attached to it. It said the same thing in three languages, English, German and French: Not today, thank you. In other words, bait recognized and refused. Whoever wrote that wasn't mad. He was still sane, still had a sense of humor, he was one of the leaders. I knew then I was close to the center, the heart of one of their buried communities. Pluck it out, I thought, and any arteries leading from it, any minor outlying limbs will perish of their own accord."

He laughed, took a large swig of brandy.

"Oh dear," he said. "I sound like Henry Messiter."

"Where?" I asked. "Where was that?"

"It had happened before," Charles said, "in a different way, but the result was the same. We saw a chap lifting the bundle. One of my men yelled at him and he hurled a grenade. Luckily it didn't explode. My man shot him. We found a piece of paper on him twisted in among the rags. Rough drawings of underground tunnels, air funnels. Another of the leaders probably. That was on the Somme. Near the village of Ginchy. What *was* Ginchy."

I felt a curious sense of excitement.

"Where was the second time? The one where they left the message?"

"You should know," he said. "You've been there, seen it. Just west of Passchendaele. Stroombeek Valley. That's our first target."

He poured more brandy into my silver cup.

"As my second in command, I thought you should know the exact location in case anything happens to me."

He looked at his watch, smiled.

"Although that's exceedingly unlikely since this ridiculous war will be over in approximately seventeen minutes. Then we can go home and start making plans to visit Stroombeek. Let's drink to that."

While we were still drinking to it, the corporal I'd last seen in the shower room at Etaples appeared in the entrance of the tent, saluted. He was a sergeant-major now but the cavalry had another name for it. "Corporal of Horse Melville," Charles said. "I believe you've met before." Melville saluted again and the colonel asked him what he wanted.

"I was just thinking, sir, that if the enemy chooses to ignore the armistice, they could cross the river out there and establish a very valuable bridgehead, sir."

"No doubt," Charles said. "Well?"

"Well, sir. The lads and I have had a bit of a discussion, and we came to the conclusion the best way of preventing that happening was to advance and occupy the area ourselves first."

He grinned suddenly.

"We've checked our watches. There's still fifteen minutes to go before eleven ack emma, sir."

It might have been the effect of the brandy but more likely, I think, that of some deep-seated atavistic need, a bugle call which only they could hear, a last chance offered for the cavalry to prove it could still ride into glory.

"Five minutes to mount," Colonel Charles said briskly, "ten minutes for the charge. Carry on, Corporal of Horse."

I watched the scene outside as the squadron swung into their saddles, stayed watching as they galloped in perfect formation, flashing past the tall trees toward the river. In spite of the drab khaki uniforms, the lack of plumes and streaming pennants, the thunder of those hooves echoed proud memories of battles long past but never forgotten, a drum roll of honor, gallantry.

Before they were halfway to their objective, the machine guns opened up, firing continuously for five minutes then ceasing abruptly at precisely eleven o'clock. The Germans too had checked their watches, and they are a people famous for their meticulous attention to detail, their obedience to orders.

The squadron had occupied the bridgehead, but by then it was decimated, half its men and horses cut to the ground. I ran forward, saw the dead body of Melville, found the colonel, one foot still caught in the stirrup of his dying horse, blood streaming from his face, the baby lips twisted in agony, the lizard eyes clouded over, expressionless. Someone was helping me to lift him. I recognized his uniform. Field grey, a German.

"This one," he said in English, "not dead." Together we carried Colonel Charles away.

The war was over.

It was over in London, too. Katherine told me afterward of the immense crowds thronging every inch of Whitehall that morning as Big Ben chimed the final stroke of the eleventh hour, of strangers embracing each other, dancing together, cheering, singing. Pieces of shredded paper rained down upon them like confetti from the buildings on either side. Even Major Askew, she said, his black glove resting on the windowsill of his office, had joined in the songs of peace.

Others, I learned later, celebrated the moment in different ways. Colonel Max von Linder, late of the Imperial German Army, stood very straight and still, staring at the barbed-wire perimeter of his prison camp in Wales, thinking of his home, if indeed it still existed. His blond hair was cut short, his face closely shaved. There was a tiny blob of dried blood on his chin, the result of a blade blunted by overuse. The nondescript uniform devoid of any badges of rank which he wore did nothing to impair his air of natural authority.

"Better get moving," his companion said. "It's a long way to London, and you know the brigadier doesn't like to be kept waiting."

Von Linder reflected on the last three days of waiting while his government, or what remained of it, came to their inevitable decision and the killing continued because the conquerors had decreed that it should. In all probability, had circumstances been different, his own people would have done the same. It was part of the insanity bred by war. He raised his hand to his chin, squeezed it thoughtfully. A small trickle of blood oozed from his shaving cut.

"I'm well aware of the brigadier's sense of punctuality," he said.

"That's good," his companion answered. "Forewarned is fore-armed, that's my motto."

Von Linder managed a weary smile. Over the past few weeks he had grown to like Captain Roy Meadows and following him now toward the guarded gate he found himself wondering how much time must pass before the host of other ex-enemies would be able to rid themselves of the bitterness and the hatred, the madness which had sustained them in the name of honor, fighting spirit.

Some, he thought sadly, never would.

Far away in a hospital in Pomerania, one of the most courageous and trusted soldiers of his regiment, a man he had recommended for the award of the Iron Cross for bravery under fire, lay in his bed temporarily blinded by gas shells. When the hospital priest entered the ward and quietly announced the news of Germany's surrender, this man wept.

Lieutenant Jean Baudroie pushed his way through the crowds in Trafalgar Square, paused as he saw the even larger ones filling Whitehall. The British national anthem rolled toward him in a great wave of sound. Lieutenant Baudroie was already late for his appointment at the War Office, but he made no attempt to move on toward it. Instead he stood to attention and began to sing The Marseillaise. Several of those around him recognized his uniform and added their voices to his. Their accents were terrible but their enthusiasm overwhelming. Lieutenant Baudroie wept too, a different kind of tears.

A few streets away Harvey James walked quickly toward his hotel. He did not feel like weeping or cheering either, simply an immense sense of relief that he could now return to his hometown and resume his normal life at the university.

"Up the Canucks!" shouted a man running past him. "God bless the Empire." Harvey James smiled. He wore the uniform of an officer in the Canadian army, but he was neither Canadian nor even a member of the British Empire. That didn't matter to him. He was in his forty-fifth year and now might well live to see his fiftieth or more. That did.

Dr. Selfridge moved slowly through the comparative calm of Harley Street, carefully observing each house, envisaging which one would eventually grace his future practice. He knew he had one final task to complete before demobilization but consoled himself that even this might provide important experience for a psychiatrist. He deeply regretted that military censorship would deprive him of the opportunity of writing a paper on it for the *Lancet*.

By nightfall the bells of London were still pealing, flags still being waved from windows darkened for years and now blazing with light, carving bright paths into a future full of hope.

CHAPTER 10

Until this night the four leaders had never been above ground at the same time. But now, summoned by Shaw, they crouched close together in the slowly drying mud and listened to the silence. It puzzled and frightened them. Silence, they had learned, was a prelude to battle, the roar of guns, death. But this silence had lasted far longer than any had done before.

They looked toward already pillaged corpses, saw no fresh ones offering sustenance. Then, full of foreboding, they descended into their sanctuary, avoided the questioning looks of the others and made their way along the tortuous passages to their special quarters, the innermost cavern.

The Acolyte, seated with his back against the wall outside it, raised unseeing eyes to them as they passed.

In London the pubs stayed open all night. Drink soothed memories of loss and pain, added excitement to new horizons of pleasure. The police issued few cautions, made even fewer arrests.

I took Colonel Charles to the nearest field hospital. He regained consciousness for a few moments between shots of morphine while waiting for the surgeons. His face was heavily bandaged, his voice very weak.

"Garrard?"

"I'm here," I said.

"Tell the headmaster I've made a bad cock-up, but make sure he knows the squadron took their objective. Don't forget that. It's an order, Garrard."

I obeyed it, returned to London as quickly as possible, reported to the brigadier.

He said nothing for a full minute, simply stared unseeingly at a heavy wooden ruler which he'd picked up from his desk and was slowly twisting in his hands. Then, suddenly, he snapped it in two as though it were no more than a brittle twig.

I'd never seen him lose control before, never known him show anger or emotion.

"The fool," he said. "The stupid, bloody, romantic fool."

He turned away, stared out of the window.

"Anthony Charles," he said quietly, "is one of the few people in this world for whom I feel a real affection."

I opened the door, making as little noise as possible.

"Even love," I heard him say as I closed it behind me.

Katherine and I went to the cinema that night. The prevailing mood in London was still one of patriotic hysteria and even there we could not entirely escape it. Before the film began, a hastily assembled message was thrown onto the screen. It came from no less a person than Sir Eric Geddes, First Lord of the Admiralty: "Who strangled all our enemies by blockade? Who drove the High Seas Fleet to mutiny? Who beat the U-boats? Who carried and protected our soldiers and food? Who saved us from invasion? THE NAVY, GOD BLESS THEM!"

A stocky broad-shouldered figure in khaki sprang to his feet three rows in front of us.

"What about the bloody army then?" he shouted and turned around, his face illuminated in the beam of the projector. "What about our boys in flaming Flanders?"

Members of the audience surrounded him from all sides, clapping him on the back, lifting him shoulder high, cheering him.

Many of them were sailors. None shouted louder than Katherine.

"Barnes!" she cried delightedly. "My one and only Fred Barnes!"

He heard her and burst clear of the clinging circle of his admirers, leaping over the intervening seats, clasping her small hands in his large ones, a huge grin spreading over his nut-brown face.

"Dr. Poole's little Katherine," he exclaimed. "Well, bless my soul!"

"Fred," she said, "dear Fred. Oh, I am so glad to see you. I thought . . . I thought perhaps . . ."

"Not me," Fred Barnes said. "They don't get rid of the Cornish so easy. They make us sergeants instead."

The film still hadn't started when we left the cinema, escorted by the more determined and vociferous of Barnes's admirers, all yelling for taxicabs to take their hero wherever he wished to go. None was available and every restaurant was full, so we walked back to our apartment, buoyed up by Katherine's promise of scrambled eggs and bacon.

It was a slow progress through the crowds and by the time we arrived I had learned a great deal about Sergeant Barnes of the Royal Engineers, born twenty-five years ago in the county town of Bodmin, a miner of china clay as his father had been before him until the day he discovered that he possessed the gift of healing, that by the laying on of hands he could cure the ills of the flesh, drive out the devils of pain and suffering.

"A century ago the old man would have been burned as a Celtic witch instead of becoming your father's partner of last resort," Barnes shouted, as we struggled through the din of the Piccadilly revelers.

"His unofficial one even then," Katherine said. "The BMA wouldn't have approved. Dad always called him his unfailing long stop, a sort of code."

Dr. Poole, it seemed, might have been the first to introduce the mystery of X rays to his practice west of the Tamar, but he was also a Cornishman and believed in other mysteries, perhaps as potent, far more ancient. Whenever modern medical science failed, he referred his patients to Barnes's father, and more often than not, Barnes's father succeeded in curing them where Dr. Poole had failed. The two men became firm friends, a relationship based on mutual respect, trust. It was natural that their children should become friends too, the high-spirited imaginative daughter of the well-to-do doctor, the down-to-earth practical son of the miner who had the magic gift. They complemented each other and both looked forward to the days when Fred Barnes wasn't working and they could roam the cliffs together, picnic in the valleys, swim in the summer seas. A difference of class, of background, never came into it. They had something more important, more lasting, in common. Each was a child of Cornwall. Fred Barnes volunteered for the army as soon as war was declared. "I'll be back for Christmas when it's all over," he told Katherine. She hadn't seen him since.

"And now you're married," he said when we eventually arrived at the apartment. "Well, all I can say is you're a lucky man, sir."

"Don't call him sir," Katherine said. "The war's over and his name's Adrian."

"He's a major," Barnes said. "Army habit."

"Acting lieutenant colonel, as a matter of fact," I said. "Have a drink, Fred."

"Whisky if you've got it, Adrian."

Katherine went to cook the bacon and eggs, and, as I suppose thousands of soldiers were doing that night, we talked about our war.

Barnes had learned how to use explosives for blasting earth out of the mines. During his first six months with the Engineers, he was trained in how to use them for blasting Germans out of the trenches. Having mastered the art, he was promoted to the rank of corporal so that he could spend the following year passing on his knowledge to others at a depot in Middlesex. "Not what I joined up for," he said, "bored to tears I was." Then in 1916 he was sent suddenly and without explanation to Flanders, to the village of Vlamertinghe a mile behind Ypres. "Knew something special was brewing as soon as I got there," he said. "The place was full of other miners. Chaps from Wales, Durham, the West Country, all over. Some drafted straight in from civilian life. Got an extra six bob a day, the lucky buggers."

I paused in the act of pouring him another whisky, knowing what was coming next.

"A general came and talked to us. I'd never seen one before. Nice bloke he was. No side. Funny little fat man with a big moustache."

"Plumer," I said, "Sir Herbert Plumer."

"That's him. Friend of yours?"

"I only saw him once," I said. "I liked him too."

Katherine put her head round the kitchen door.

"Ready in two minutes," she called. "Lay the table."

Barnes and I dodged round each other, inexpertly arranging knives and forks, raffia mats, glasses.

"You tunneled right under their lines, didn't you," I said. "Mined the lot. Messines Ridge up to Hill 60."

Barnes looked surprised. "You were in the salient too?"

"Above ground, not under it."

"Took the best part of a year," he said. "Don't think we'd ever have finished if it hadn't been for old Plumer. Kept sending messages. 'Be patient, lads, keep at it. We'll get there in the end.'"

"You did," I said.

Katherine came in with the food. Lacking the brigadier's champagne, I opened bottles of beer.

"Lovely grub," Barnes said. "She always was a great cook, your wife. Remember those picnics?"

"Hot pasties with cold cider," Katherine said. "Very wicked."

"Were you working under the Messines Ridge?" I asked Barnes.

"Oh, no," Katherine exclaimed in mock horror, "not more old soldiers' reminiscences, *please*."

Barnes grinned at her, shook his head.

"Hill 60," he said. "That right old bugger."

They had started by sinking camouflaged shafts down into the heavy brown mud, through more water and sand, deep into the hard blue clay sixty feet or more beneath the surface. Then the tunneling began, clawing forward inch by inch toward the enemy lines, eight men to each shift, six hours on, eighteen off, half working at the face with picks or sharp pointed spades, the others following, filling innumerable sandbags with the displaced clay, carrying them back to the foot of the shaft, a journey increasing in length by a few feet each day. The sandbags, winched up from below, could only be removed and scattered at night for fear the German lookouts would see them, guess their purpose, perhaps shell them just to make sure. It was a slow back-breaking progress, halted every yard or so while the walls of the tunnels were shored up with timbers. Each was less than five feet high, not quite three feet wide. Many were blown up by countermining enemy sappers, and fresh ones had to be driven through to take their place.

"When a tunnel falls in behind you sixty feet down," Barnes said, "that's it. No way out. Good-bye, chum."

They were equipped with geophones, a sort of subterranean

stethoscope which, when placed against the clay, enabled them to listen to the Germans probing in the opposite direction, trying to locate their whereabouts, anticipate their intentions. Sometimes they managed to destroy these intruders before they were themselves destroyed. For this purpose they used small mines known as camouflets.

"Did you ever play a nursery game called Murder?" Barnes asked. "All the kids hiding in the dark, scared stiff, trying not to get spotted by the killer. It reminded me of that, only there was no end to it. Moles we were down there, blind moles, scared stiffer than any kid." When the tunnel at Hill 60, like those of the others to the south, had been completed, the carefully cleared space at the end of it, the final chamber, had to be filled with explosives. It was brought up in fifty-pound bags of ammonal, each carried by one man, and these were packed tightly together in the chambers, their fuse wires trailed back through the tunnels to the firing positions. More sandbags were jammed around them so that when the explosion took place, its force would not be dissipated laterally, but concentrated directly upward toward the destruction of the enemy above.

"No wonder it took a year," Barnes said and grinned. "Seemed more like ten."

He told us all of this in a matter-of-fact unemotional fashion, an expert recalling a difficult but necessary, and ultimately successful, experiment.

Katherine took away our empty plates, returned with coffee.

"There were rumors," I said to Barnes, "that near Hill 60 some of you could actually hear the voices of Germans burrowing alongside you."

"I never heard any Germans myself," Barnes said, "but I knew a few that did."

He sipped his coffee appreciatively, smiled at Katherine.

"The real stuff, this. How did you come to find it?"

"My husband works at the War Office," Katherine said. "There are perks. Quite disgraceful."

She took her cup, moved to the armchair, sank into it.

"Bags the only decent seat."

"Lady's privilege," Barnes said.

"Don't be so prewar and old-fashioned, Fred. It's the cook's. The cook's and the washer-up's."

Barnes and I lit cigarettes, sat back in our own chairs. No one spoke for a minute or two. There was no need. I think we all felt happy to be together, relaxed, comfortable, friends. I know I did.

"Funny you should ask me that," Barnes said suddenly. "About hearing chaps speak German under the ground out there."

"Why funny?"

"I heard some speaking in English," Barnes said, "but they weren't on the same level as us. They were deeper down."

Katherine leaned forward in her chair. I could feel her alertness, her tension.

"Probably another section of your tunnelers," I said.

Barnes shook his head. "There were no others out that night. I checked."

"You're sure?" Katherine asked.

"As sure as I sit here, my dear."

I hesitated before asking my next question, glanced at Katherine. She nodded.

"Did you do anything about it?" I asked Barnes. "Tell anyone else?"

"I told my CO, Captain Stevens. He said he'd report it."

"And did he?"

"I don't know. He was killed the next night. Shrapnel hit a bag of ammonal while he was trying to assemble it."

Barnes's face was drawn, haunted with memory.

The whole atmosphere of the room had changed, become filled with other ghosts, other memories.

"He was a good bloke," Barnes said.

He got up, shaking his head, then his whole body as a dog will do to rid itself of water, of arcane fears perhaps, forced a smile, asked Katherine if he might have another cup of War Office coffee.

"I clean forgot about those blokes talking English," he said. "Never gave it another thought, not till now. What you said reminded me somehow."

Katherine poured his coffee.

"The timing of words," she said, "often has more effect than the words themselves."

I was puzzled, but Barnes understood at once.

"That's what my dad used to say. Fancy you remembering."

He turned to me, explained. "He'd always tell his patients

that. It wasn't just his hands he used. His voice as well. When he was healing scars and suchlike."

"There are scars and scars," Katherine said, "and there are different means of healing them."

I decided then what I was going to do.

"What are your plans now it's over?" I asked Barnes. "Will you stay in the army?"

"Reckon it'd be a bit on the dull side, but I might for a while if they want me." He glanced at Katherine. "Not much doing in the china clay trade from all I hear."

I felt it wiser not to say any more until I'd spoken to the brigadier. After that it would be up to Barnes.

When he'd left, Katherine said, "I'm sure he'll accept and I can't think of anyone who'd be more useful to have with you. He's thorough and he's loyal and he knows his job, does our Fred."

"That's much the same as Messiter said about you."

"We're very special people, the Cornish," Katherine said as we got into bed. "A touch psychic, perhaps."

CHAPTER 11

The brigadier's away on a trip to the continent," the subaltern said, managing to make the news sound casual and mysterious at the same time. He had relinquished his uniform in favor of a well-cut civilian suit and an old Harrovian tie. Furthermore, I noted, the battlefields had already become the continent once again. In spite of constant rumors to the contrary, it was clear that the armistice was holding, that peace had really begun. I asked when the brigadier was expected back.

"That depends what happens in Paris," the subaltern said and grinned confidentially as though referring to a dirty weekend.

Major Askew was hardly more informative. "I imagine it may have something to do with setting up arrangements for the peace conference. He said he might be bringing an old friend back with him."

I knew exactly who that would be.

Neither Askew nor I mentioned any future plans the brigadier had in store for us, certainly in my case, and presumably in his, because neither was sure that the other had been informed of them. We returned without enthusiasm to the pretense of completing our spurious lists of suspects and trusties.

I wrote the brigadier a memorandum on the subject of Sergeant Frederick Barnes and put it in an envelope marked "Secret."

A fortnight later, on the day of his return, I received a note from him informing me that in view of Colonel Charles's incapacity I was to take command of the Stroombeek operation.

On the following morning he summoned me to his room. Two men were leaving by the inner door as I entered from the passage. I saw only their backs as they started down the staircase, but this time I was sure. One of them I'd already seen driving the brigadier's car. Roy Meadows.

"I've decided to designate those we are seeking the men of Golgotha," the brigadier said before I could speak. "I mean it in no blasphemous sense, Garrard, no reference intended to the tribulations of our Lord. The name you understand derives from the Hebrew word *golgoleth* meaning skull. Hence its literal meaning— a place of burial. Particularly apt, I'm sure you'll agree. That is where our men are. In a burial place of their own choosing. It differs from others only in that it still harbors life."

He waved a piece of paper at me, transferred it from a hollowed-out shell case on the right-hand side of his desk to another on the left. In a more conventional office they might have been described as in and out trays.

"When the cat's away," he said, "a great deal of milk is apt to accumulate in his saucer. I've just been dealing with this written request remarkably similar to your own. An officer petitioning for the services of an NCO from his old regiment. Forgive me keeping you waiting. I had to see him first as his free time and movements are necessarily subject to strict limitations. He's a German prisoner of war. Major Max von Linder."

"Escorted by Captain Meadows of the military police," I said flatly.

He showed no surprise.

"Recognized him, did you? No harm done. You'll be seeing a lot of each other in the future. As you know, I like keeping certain matters in the family. To those already in the know. Prudent. Helpful."

I kept my temper with difficulty.

"It would be even more helpful, sir, if you'd tell me just who is going with me."

"Well, Meadows and von Linder for a start, assuming I can secure an early release for him. And, I very much hope, his NCO if we can find him. Apparently he acted as one of the regimental runners. In the course of his duties when they were in the Ypres salient, he not only saw the men of Golgotha on several occasions, but drew accurate and detailed maps of his sightings. Von Linder forwarded them to his superiors. They felt it wiser to suppress and ignore them for the same reasons as our own high command. But the NCO kept copies. If he still has them, they would be of great value in combination with the information supplied by Colonel Charles. One might say of vital importance."

"Who is this NCO?" I asked.

"A corporal. Unfortunately von Linder cannot remember his name but I have that of his regiment and a physical description. Inquiries have been started."

"Two probables and one possible," I said. "Is that all?"

He smiled, the cautionary model.

"By no means. Have patience. All will be revealed in due course."

He opened a thick file which lay on the desk between the shell cases. "Now, as to your Sergeant Barnes. This document contains names and dates relating to all reports in any way connected with the existence or otherwise of the men of Golgotha."

Like the rest, it bore no written title, simply a code of figures.

"Some day soon," he said thoughtfully, "I suppose we shall have to select a name for your forthcoming expedition. Civilians in high places dislike sanctioning secret operations unless they have one. The simpler the better. A name affords a sense of propriety, calms doubts. Once accepted, it tends to forestall further irritating inquiries."

He leafed quickly through the file.

"Not that in this instance I anticipate the necessity of acquainting many of them with precise details. Perhaps only one. Possibly none at all."

He was examining the section headed S.

"Ah, yes, here we are. Stevens. Captain Lionel Stevens, MC. On April 29th, 1917, he reported that one of his tunnelers had heard English voices in the vicinity of Hill 60 by means of a geophone. No other Allied tunneling parties were present in the area at that time. Name of informant—Sergeant Frederick Barnes. Quite correct, Garrard."

He looked up at me and smiled, a headmaster pleased with his pupil. "There is a red tick against the captain's name," he said, "indicating that he was killed in action."

"The next day," I said. "Barnes told me."

His finger moved smoothly across the page.

"April thirtieth. Correct again."

He snapped the file shut.

"There are a very large number of red ticks in these records," he said. "Regrettable, of course, but their prevalence does serve to render the whole question of Golgotha less manifest, more secure."

He might just as well, I thought, have said that dead men tell no tales and left it at that.

"What happened to Stevens's report?" I asked.

"As with the others," he said, "noted, filed. Otherwise officially ignored." He switched on the desk lamp. Its light fractured against his impenetrable lenses. "Until now, that is," he added.

"When we go," I said, "I want Barnes to come with us."

"Quite so. You make that plain in your written memorandum. I'll see about it. There's still adequate time. Our troops have not yet completed crossing the German frontier. Until they do, it would be premature to assume the battlefields are ready to accommodate our particular investigations."

He produced an unexpected grin, the roguish model.

"One must ensure the field of play is clear before beginning the game."

"It's not a game," I said angrily.

He looked immediately penitent.

"Forgive me, Garrard. A poor joke."

He pushed back his chair, picked up the file, locked it away in a steel cabinet. "And yet," he said, "it perhaps provides a clue as to an appropriately temperate operational code name. Soothing. In the English sporting tradition. What would you say to the Golgotha Game?"

The inner door opened before I could answer and Colonel Charles stood there, his left arm supported by a clean white sling, a livid scar running across his forehead. Beneath it, the lizard eyes seemed even colder, more remote than before. Otherwise he hadn't changed, still perfectly groomed, parade-ground spruce.

The brigadier greeted him warmly.

"My dear Anthony. Lieutenant Colonel Garrard and I were just discussing a possible title for the Golgotha operation."

"My successor in command," Charles said. "Be more careful than I was, Garrard." There was no welcome in his eyes.

"I brought Anthony back from Paris with me," the brigadier said and went over to him and took him by the arm.

"Quite unnecessary," Charles said. "I was perfectly capable of getting here on my own."

Messiter guided him to a chair and it was then that I was absolutely sure. Colonel Charles was blind.

"How about the Golgotha Game?" the brigadier asked him cheerfully.

"Appalling bad taste, Henry."

"But secure, don't you think? Comfortingly vague and misleading. Besides I rather favor the alliteration."

The colonel twisted his head in my direction.

"Why so silent, Garrard? Speak up. Say something."

"It's good to see you again, sir," I said and at once regretted the choice of verb.

"That's better," Charles said. "Now I know where you are. How's your attractive wife?"

I told him that Katherine was in fine form and would be delighted to know that he was safe and well. The last word, I knew, was the wrong one again.

"A gamble," he said suddenly.

I thought he was referring to my marriage, then that perhaps he meant the cavalry charge at Maubeuge. Even the brigadier seemed taken by surprise. The colonel stared at him with sightless eyes, smiled with rosebud lips.

"Speaking as one of its godfathers and respecting your penchant for alliteration, Henry, I would like to propose an alternative christening for the baby. Equally secure, but to the initiated far more appropriate and descriptive from whichever angle you choose to regard it. The hunted or the hunter's. Theirs or ours."

We waited, the brigadier with his pencil poised.

"The Golgotha Gamble," Colonel Charles said.

And so, from that moment on, it became.

"Fred Barnes telephoned," Katherine said when I came home a week later. "He's been in London for a couple of days visiting St. Dunstan's. They wanted someone to help teach the people there how to move around in the dark and he was chosen. Because of all his experience in those dreadful tunnels, I suppose."

I took the glass of whisky she had waiting for me, drank it slowly.

"I'm sure he did a good job," I said.

"And enjoyed doing it," she said. "There was a blind colonel there and apparently they got on famously, had quite a chat. He's invited Fred out to dinner at his club tonight. Fred's so excited you'd think he was going to Buckingham Palace."

The brigadier, as usual, had wasted no time, either in seeing about it or keeping it well within the family.

Blind men, I thought, make good listeners, particularly when they've been previously trained for the job like Anthony Charles.

"New Year's Eve, gentlemen," the brigadier said, gazing round the table, enveloping all of us in his favorite smile, the benevolent model. "A time for friendly gatherings, good fellowship. Above all, one for fresh resolutions, carving a brighter future from a tarnished past, strong, firm, dedicated."

Dinner was over, the club waiters had withdrawn and both doors of the big room in Carlton House Terrace were locked. There was no fear of interruption and he had clearly decided to make the most of his opportunity. Perhaps the two hours he had spent in Downing Street earlier that evening were lending additional color to his speech. Perhaps he'd simply had too much port. He refilled his glass, passed the decanter to me on his left and continued.

"In rather less than three weeks, the leaders of the Allied powers will assemble in Paris for the peace conference. Their task is no less than to build a new world, more specifically a new Europe. You, gentlemen, humbler but no less important representatives of different nations—you are in the special position of knowing that such a new Europe can only safely rest, quite literally, on foundations which are sound and secure. Those foundations must therefore be cleansed of pestilence, of putrefaction, of the lurking but potent germs of decay with which they are still contaminated. I speak of the carrion, the wild lawless banditry which continue to infest them, and I repeat, I speak literally. Those foundations, that scarred earth must, like the Augean stables, be scoured, purged, made clean."

All the oratorial stops were out, but I decided it had nothing to do with the port. He'd weighed up his audience, knew the French and German officers, at least, would respond to a few high-flown

phrases even when modified by Askew's whispered translations of
the more esoteric references. But the rest seemed to be enjoying
the performance too and so was I. The brigadier's aim was as always
on target. After ten days of hard incisive briefing, a little entertain-
ment was in order. After the rigors of the stick, the pleasurable
presentation of the carrot.

Three weeks before the dinner, he had informed me that
Askew had been assigned to me as an interpreter. "Your other
officers will report to you tomorrow. They have already been told of
the general plan. Once you have met and approved them, we shall
proceed to detailed briefing. It will be thorough, take time.
Everyone must be fully prepared. No margin for errors."

"Sergeant Barnes?" I asked.

"Already on the strength. Anthony Charles was most impressed with him."

"He was most impressed with the colonel's dinner," I said.
"He'd never been to the Cavalry Club before."

Next day, in a room at the war office specially set aside for the
purpose, the subaltern, now back in uniform, perhaps in honor of
the occasion, had presented each of my officers in turn and then left
us alone together until I pressed the buzzer for him to bring in the
next. Two of them I already knew. Selfridge and Roy Meadows. "I
was most careful to make it clear that I did not disbelieve you,"
Selfridge said after he had made solicitous inquiries about my leg.
"I simply expressed the hope that you would soon forget the
experience. That was no less than my medical duty."

He was still being careful, I realized. I wanted to remind him
that he'd told Captain Bates that what I had seen was pure fantasy, a
trick of the mind, that his testimony might have sent Sergeant
Wilkins to face a firing squad. But Bates was dead and so now was
Wilkins and I held my peace.

"I'm aware, of course," he said, "that I was originally selected
for this particular duty because I was mentioned as being au
courant with the facts of your sergeant's court-martial, but I feel
relatively certain that a subsequent investigation of my psychiatric
background implemented their final decision."

He didn't enquire the final decision of the court-martial. A
careful man indeed.

Meeting Roy Meadows again was considerably more pleasant.
"There I was," he said, "happily doing my bit to stem the German

hordes and generally minding my own business when I'm suddenly yanked out of the line and told to report home for special duties."

"Once a policeman always a policeman, Roy."

"How's the lovely Katherine?"

"She's fine."

"Any kids yet?"

"Give us a chance. There's one on the way, as a matter of fact." It seemed appropriate that he should be the first person I'd told.

"You'll like my kraut friend," he said, "the one I've been sort of looking after. Major Linder with a von in front. He's all right. Just one thing, though. Don't mention the last three days' fighting while his chaps were deciding whether to surrender or not. That really upsets him."

"Thanks," I said. "Forewarned is forearmed."

Meadows was right. I liked Max von Linder from the moment we met.

"I've seen what you have seen, colonel," he said. "One kind of madness created by a bigger madness. Perhaps we may help remove it together?"

He might have prepared the speech, but I didn't think so. There was the merest suggestion of humor in his very blue eyes but there was something else too, immediately recognizable. The look shared by all who had experienced for too long the horror of the trenches, the pervading presence of useless death.

He spoke English with a slight accent, otherwise almost perfectly.

"Before the war," he said, "I passed many holidays in your country. I enjoyed most the part which leads to what you call Land's End."

"Cornwall?"

"Yes," he said, "Cornwall. The coasts remind me a little of my home near Kiel in Schleswig-Holstein. But the water is warmer. Not cold like the North Sea." He smiled. "Perhaps the people also."

"My wife's Cornish," I said. I told him about Barnes too, his expertise as a miner.

"There's another man I hope will be joining us," he said. "I am ashamed not to remember his name because he was one of the bravest, the most loyal, in my regiment."

The haunted look was back in his eyes.

"Sometimes I think one remembers best the names of the dead. Those to whom one can no longer call."

I knew exactly what he meant. Wilkins, Richardson, many many more. "The brigadier's told me about him," I said. "He drew maps, plans."

Von Linder nodded. "If he's still alive, he must be in Germany now. I hope very much that the brigadier's inquiries are successful."

"They usually are," I said.

Lieutenant Baudroie was next, his French formality not quite concealing his impatience, a suppressed aggression. He spoke English with difficulty and I'd had to call on the interpretive services of Edward Askew. We talked of his countryman whom the brigadier had agreed should accompany him, another mining and explosives expert like Barnes.

"He's excellent at his work," Askew translated, "but an ordinary soldier, not of the officer type."

France, I thought, in spite of its revolution in the name of equality and fraternity, could still be a remarkably class-conscious country.

"The lieutenant thinks we have waited long enough," Askew said. "He is eager to begin the operation without further delay."

I saw the expression in Baudroie's deep-set brown eyes. Anger, hatred. The sort of look we had been taught to adopt in the trenches when going over the top. The killer look.

"Tell him," I said equably, "that the English are a cautious people. We believe in the importance of making adequate preparations."

He must have understood the gist of this because he answered quickly and emphatically before Askew had an opportunity to intervene.

"For the French," he translated, "it is different."

I asked why and had no need of Askew's help to understand the answer.

"England has not been invaded. France has."

The same old mistrust, I thought. Still inviolate and therefore perfidious Albion. The ally who will fight to the last French soldier. But I had, in large part, misjudged him.

"The bastards we seek defile the soil of his country," Askew translated, "and many of them are Frenchmen."

Baudroie's angry tone, his flushed cheeks, left little doubt as to their fate should he be the first to find them.

I felt it invidious to point out that the Stroombeek valley was in fact in Belgium, but by the time we came to exchange courteous au revoirs, I had decided it would be necessary to keep a watchful eye on the lieutenant.

The brigadier had assured me there would be no need of an interpreter for Captain Harvey James.

He sat back easily in his chair, took a fat cigar from the breast pocket of his Canadian uniform, and grinned.

"I'm a phoney," he said, "not a Canuck at all. Just a Yank from Illinois. Henry Messiter flushed me out. Blew my cover. Guess it takes one to know one. Well, that's why I'm here."

He lit the cigar, blew out a stream of smoke, then looked unexpectedly flustered, apologetic.

"Sorry, colonel. Should have asked your okay before lighting up?"

"Don't worry," I said. "I like the smell." He was at least twenty years older than me.

"My dad's real full-blooded Ivy League American. Drop dead rather than vote Democrat. But he understood. He saw what was coming. You want to go, he said. Okay, why wait? I'd have volunteered for your army except they'd have spotted the accent a mile away. It was easier with the Canadians. Easier still after what happened to them in April '15. Reckon they thought I might be of some real use after that."

I had read the brigadier's notes on his background. "The first gas attack at Ypres?"

"Right. I'm a research chemist back home, you see. I study stuff like that at the university. Germs, chemical warfare, you name it. You think that's a pretty goddam awful way to earn a living?"

"Depends how you use the knowledge," I said.

"Prevention's better than cure, colonel, but to prevent you've got to know just that little bit extra than the guys who're spreading the germs."

"We've spread quite a few in our turn, one way and another," I said.

He shrugged. "That's war," he said, "the name of the game. Always has been right through history. First the bow and arrow, then the chain mail. X invents a new weapon, Y comes up with a better one by way of protection, only it doesn't stop there. X and Y keep beating their brains out to make sure they can beat the hell out of each other. Always will be, I guess, till maybe one day they'll each discover something so goddam frightening they'll both be too terrified to use it. That'll fuck up the equation. They might even have to learn how to live in peace with each other. Homo getting sapiens the hard way." He gave a wide grin. "Sorry," he said. "Typical scientist's excuse for sins of commission."

In the next few minutes he told me a lot about the various forms and uses of poison gas, the initial fear and panic they engendered, the first pathetic attempts at safeguards against them, such as silk stockings cut into strips and soaked in urine, the amazing ignorance which led some regiments to advance in the wake of one of their own chlorine attacks without protective masks, forgetting that the wind might change direction at any moment.

The cylinders he would be bringing to Stroombeek valley, he explained, contained gas of the very latest type, easy to control and direct, immediately lethal.

I told him I hoped it wouldn't be necessary to use them. He nodded, his expression serious, and for the first time I saw that same haunted look.

"A buddy of mine, real close—one night out on wire patrol he ran into a bunch of those ghouls we're after. Drove him crazy. Finished up in a nut house. So I've got every reason to hate 'em. But Jesus Christ, colonel, you don't hope it as much as I do—not even for them."

He gave me one of his cigars before leaving. I knew I wouldn't smoke it, but gifts are a part of friendship and mine with Harvey James had only just begun.

Intensive briefing sessions conducted by the brigadier and Colonel Charles started the next day. As near as possible exact locations, weather conditions, modes of transport, weapons, living quarters, communications, code words, medical arrangements. There were two other NCOs besides Barnes, one English, one French, both former miners. They supplied much detailed techni-cal information to do with working underground, answered many questions ranging from methods of testing for foul air to the best means of shoring up tunnels.

By the time the sessions were completed, all concerned knew everything that was required of them. Everything, that is, with the exception of precisely how to detain and arrest an unspecified number of men in varying stages of mental instability who had been living a clandestine troglodyte life for several years. No one could provide advice on that because no one had ever done it before.

"In the unlikely event of your being questioned as to where you're going or what you're doing, your answer will be that you're an advance party of the war graves commission. Is that clear?"

Selfridge was the only one who laughed, and as no one else did, he immediately suppressed it.

"Quite clear," he said loudly.

"One final question," the brigadier said. "If any of you feel like changing your minds, resigning from the operation, say so now. There'll be no criticism, no recriminations. I don't pretend it's going to be a picnic."

No one spoke.

Then came the dinner.

I had insisted to the brigadier that Barnes and the other two NCOs should attend it. From the outset I was determined that my group, within the limits of military discipline, should be run as nearly as possible on democratic lines.

I watched their faces as the port completed its circuit in front of Colonel Charles, who sat quietly on the other side of the brigadier listening to the closing passages of his peroration. Meadows and von Linder looked politely bored, Baudroie impatient. Edward Askew appeared exhausted by his efforts at translation, Selfridge was nodding his head in an approving if somewhat condescending manner, and Harvey James kept fingering his unlit cigar as though someone had told him he should resist smoking before the Loyal Toast. The expressions of Barnes and his two colleagues were clear to read. Who cares how long the red-tabbed old bugger rambles on so long as the booze keeps coming? Only Colonel Charles seemed to find his friend's performance at all amusing. But even that must have been a trick of the light. Blind eyes can't smile.

"Root them out, bring them to justice," concluded the brigadier. "That will be your task in the Stroombeek Valley. Are your glasses charged, gentlemen?"

An affirmative buzz indicated that they were. Messiter lifted his own, his gaze sweeping round the whole table, a headmaster happy with the end-of-term results, about to announce the prize-giving.

"To the success of your endeavors in the Golgotha Gamble," he said. We rose to our feet and drank.

Harvey James lit his cigar.

Although not due to sail till the following evening, we were, apparently, officially launched, on our way.

Later, as we were all preparing to leave, the telephone specially installed on a side table gave a discreet buzz. The brigadier lifted the receiver, listened for a few moments, then guided Colonel Charles to a corner of the room, beckoned von Linder and myself to join them. "Stay awhile," he said. "One of my people has arrived from Germany. A Lieutenant Vallance. He has news for us."

Ten minutes after the others had gone, Vallance came into the room. He looked tired but pleased with himself, still alert like a retriever bringing back the right bird at the end of a long day.

"Speak," said the brigadier.

Vallance produced a notebook from his hip pocket, took a deep breath, spoke in a rapid monotone.

"Captain Barton and I have found Major von Linder's NCO in Munich. He apparently reported to the adjutant of the regiment's reserve battalion there on being discharged from the hospital after temporary blindness incurred by exposure to a gas attack. We spoke first to the adjutant, gave him a verbal description of the man. He identified him at once, but before sending for him warned us that he had been engaged on covert work of a dangerous nature."

"Warned?" said von Linder as Vallance took another breath before continuing.

"We were told he was engaged in an undercover capacity spying on Red elements in the army, compiling dossiers with which to discredit them at the appropriate time."

"Good," von Linder said.

Vallance looked apologetically at the brigadier. "Your instructions were not to involve ourselves in their internal politics, sir, so we didn't press for further details in that line."

"Quite right, my boy. Carry on."

"The adjutant was reluctant to give us the man's name,"

Vallance said. "Perhaps he thought we might report him to the authorities."

"Don't conjecture," Colonel Charles said sharply. "Just the facts."

"Captain Barton assured the adjutant our inquiries bore no relation to the present situation in Germany. That they were of a personal nature and emanated from a prisoner of war in England." He shot von Linder a quick glance. "Yourself, sir."

"The man's name," von Linder said impatiently. "Did he tell you his name?"

"Not at once, sir. But he sent for him and ordered him to give it to us himself." Vallance looked down at his notes.

"'Polzl,' the man said. 'My name is Polzl, Corporal Polzl.'"

"Polzl?" von Linder repeated. He gave it the correct German pronunciation but looked puzzled.

"That's what he said, sir."

"Did the adjutant say anything?" asked the brigadier.

"No, sir. He just nodded."

He looked at von Linder again. "We told the corporal that you might wish to get in touch with him, sir, and he immediately became interested. Animated wouldn't be too strong a word. 'I'd do anything for Major von Linder,' he said. He obviously remembers you very well, sir."

The brigadier glanced quickly at von Linder.

"Don't worry, my dear chap. I often forget my own people's names. Forget yours sometimes, don't I, Vallance?"

Lieutenant Vallance, reorganizing a question which could not be satisfactorily answered with either a positive or a negative, wisely remained silent.

"Photograph," asked the brigadier.

"Here, sir." Vallance produced it from the back of his notebook. I looked at it over von Linder's shoulder. A thin face with prominent ears, a long moustache waxed and upturned at either end, the eyes resentful, angry. Well, no one engaged in his sort of activity would welcome his picture being taken.

"That's him," von Linder said with relief and certainty. "Polzl. How could I forget such a name?"

"No time to have him sent here," the brigadier said. "He'll rendezvous with you at Ypres."

"How will he get there?"

"We'll see to it," Charles said.

"You are sure it can be managed?"

"Of course it can," the colonel said. "Dammit man, we won the bloody war didn't we?"

"Only just," said Max von Linder and we all laughed with him.

CHAPTER 12

The boat nosed into the port of Calais. No crews manned the anti-aircraft guns, no searchlights probed the night sky. It was apparently once more the unguarded gateway to a country officially at peace, but, as we knew from our briefings, one still jammed with foreign soldiers whose declared aim was to get out of it, return to their own homes, some even prepared to risk mutiny to accelerate the process. I moved round the deck making sure that my men were all in civilian clothes, their uniforms packed away out of sight in suitcases. Each carried a specially prepared pass identifying him as a member of the War Graves Commission. Fragments of their conversations drifted toward me.

"They say President Wilson's coming over for the peace conference," Harvey James said to Baudroie. "I can't pretend I like him but he's a tough guy in an argument."

Askew stood between them, twisting his head like a tennis umpire as he translated back and forth.

"Baudroie considers President Clemenceau will gobble him up for breakfast," he said.

Harvey James grinned. "In that case tell him the old boy'll likely die of food poisoning. Woodrow Wilson's a Democrat."

Barnes emerged from the deck below. He was carrying von Linder's case as well as his own. The German thanked him and they both looked over the rail toward the brightly lit dockyard.

"I wonder what the British would have done," von Linder said, "if we had managed to capture the French channel ports."

"Landed in sunny Italy and booted the kaiser up the arse from there, I suppose," Barnes answered cheerfully, adding the word "sir" to ensure that the major didn't think he was merely trying to be rude.

Von Linder was amused. "You'll get on well with my Corporal Polzl," he said. "He never imagined for one moment the war could be lost either."

"I can get on with anyone who likes a good joke," Barnes said.

Roy Meadows was talking to Selfridge.

"Given a bit of luck, they'll all be dead from starvation by the time we find them. Even the military police aren't expected to arrest skeletons."

"Not all," Selfridge assured him. "Certainly not all."

"Why so sure, doctor?"

"Whatever food they've already got can be stored. Cold down there. Natural refrigeration. Besides there are turnip roots, that sort of thing." His tone was matter of fact, clinical.

Meadows grunted. "Lovely grub. What happens when all that runs out?"

"They'll still have each other," Selfridge said. "In extremis, that is."

Meadows stared at him.

"Cannibalism," Selfridge explained. He might have been pointing out the symptoms of a sprained ankle to a lay patient. Just another medical fact.

I moved on past the other two NCOs who were arguing about the relative merits of French and English beer, joined Katherine in the bows. She alone, not being an official member of our party, was in uniform, her nurse's dress and cape. "If you do send me any wounded," she said, "please make sure you're not one of them. I couldn't go through all that again."

We weren't supposed to be seen talking to one another, but there was a limit to security, even that imposed by the brigadier.

"I love you," I said.

She squeezed my fingers in hers, not looking at me.

"Please don't take any risks, but don't waste any time either. I'm three months' pregnant. We'd prefer him to be born in England, wouldn't we?"

"He will be. You can be sure of that. I'd better go now."

"Be very careful," she said as I turned away. "I love you too."

Two lorries were waiting when we docked. I stood beside them while they were loaded with our gear. It included four metal crates to which Harvey James paid special attention. A soldier lurched past us on his way to the ship, his face unshaven, his breath heavy with the smell of brandy, a man who didn't care anymore, a man going home.

"What the blazes you got in there?"

"Gravestones," James told him. "Prototype models."

"You'll need a lot more than that, mate," the soldier said. "A hell of a lot more."

An ambulance entered the docks, stopped a few yards away. Men on stretchers were carried from it to the ship. The war might be over but not its wounds and many would never be healed.

When the ambulance had been emptied, Katherine got in beside the driver. I tried not to look as it moved away, but at least managed not to wave farewell.

Beside me, Fred Barnes said very quietly, "Don't you worry, Adrian. You'll be together again soon." Then he shouted in his best sergeant's manner, "All loaded up now, sir. Permission to get started?"

I climbed into the front passenger seat of the first lorry and we followed the ambulance out of the docks. It turned to the right at the first crossroads in the town, and as our small convoy kept straight on, I glimpsed its taillights with the faintly illuminated red cross above them as it carried Katherine away from me toward Le Touquet.

In the Stroombeek valley the Shouter always wore his watch. Its hands had long since disappeared and its works were rusted solid but it was, even so, still a watch. He kept it only because the other leaders had told him that he should. When they were below ground, in the innermost cavern, separated from the others by a curtain of two layers of heavy sacking, the four of them talked in a mixture of their own languages, not the one which belonged to none of them and which they employed to call to each other on the surface. Down there they had told him to keep the watch because it was something which made him different from the rest. No one else had a watch. Shaw had a metal disc on a piece of string which he

kept wound tightly round his wrist, the Marksman had the likeness
of a sad-faced lady tattooed on his right arm, and the Priest had a
wooden cross hanging from a leather strap around his neck. Each of
these objects had a name, an identity. None of the others had
anything to mark them as being different. But Shaw with St.
Christopher, the Marksman with Holy Mother, the Priest with our
Savior and the Shouter with his watch, they were different. So the
Shouter always wore it.

He crouched now under the stars, gulping in the night air,
listening to the silence of the valley. It had been silent for a long
time. Between them the leaders had counted the nights. Fifty of
them without the roar of the guns, thirty with no sound at all since
the soldiers had left. The Shouter couldn't understand why or how
they had all gone like that, none screaming, none falling, not a
single one remaining to be plundered, but Shaw had explained at
the time that it must be a trap, and the Priest and the Marksman
had agreed, and he had known they must be right. All the world
above them was a trap waiting for them to walk into it. Every one of
them knew that, even the others who were not, like the four of
them, different.

In spite of this the Shouter found that he enjoyed the silence.
It made thinking easier, remembering. He thought increasingly
now of the village called Lambach, remembered more clearly the
monastery where he had sung in the choir. Were they still there,
would he ever see them again? The strangeness of these thoughts
and memories surprised and frightened him. He realized that he
actually wanted to escape from their refuge, to join once more the
world they had renounced. He would have to confess this heresy to
his fellow leaders, seek their counsel.

He climbed down the shaft into the central area where the
others lived, moved slowly through the network of low passages,
passed a heavy sheet of metal which blocked the entrance to a small
unoccupied cavern. It had once been part of the side armor of a
tank and concealed the place where Shaw and the Marksman kept
their supply of guns and ammunition. The Acolyte crouched on the
flattened earth outside it. The Shouter patted him on the head,
went on toward the sacking curtain which hid the leaders' cavern.

He had expected them to be surprised at least, more probably
angry. But they weren't. It seemed they had been asking themselves the same sort of questions and to an extent had begun to

answer them. That was why, Shaw and the Marksman told him, they had been keeping the others busy filling in and blocking off so many of their exit tunnels. The principal two which remained would be quite sufficient for their needs. It would be stupid to leave unnecessary evidence of their former presence once they were gone. Gone? The Shouter couldn't take it in, couldn't believe it. They were going? Actually going? Going where?

The war, the Priest explained, must have ended. The killing, God be thanked, must be at an end.

A single thought thrust itself to the forefront of the Shouter's confused mind. God might have stopped the killing, but even God could not make the world outside safe for them, those who had chosen to flout its rules, live by their own. But the Priest was still talking.

If the silence persisted for another seven nights, they would start to leave. Not all at once, but in small groups. He would explain to the others. Once they had reached the surface, each man would decide for himself what he must do, where he must go. But whatever they did, wherever they went, it must be in the name of peace. He would advise that they should tell the simple truth, that they had chosen to live in peace rather than continue to kill those who had done them no harm simply because they bore the label "enemy." The world itself was living in peace now, there were no more enemies. So the world would surely not turn them away. Even those whose nature had been to demand sacrifice would surely find in their hearts understanding, forgiveness for them who had lived by forgiving.

His voice rose in a shout of triumph as he reached for the cup and the bread.

"Be ye not afraid," he said. "God will provide."

"I will keep my gun," the Marksman said.

Shaw said nothing, but the Shouter saw that he was twisting St. Christopher with the fingers of his left hand.

"Holy Communion?" asked the Priest.

No one answered.

CHAPTER 13

Where are you taking me?" Corporal Polzl asked. The adjutant had told him it was quite safe to make the journey, assured him that its purpose was to reunite him with his former commanding officer, Major von Linder, who would have work for him to do, important work. But he could specify neither its nature nor the name of the place where they would meet because the British hadn't told him either of those things. "We must trust them," the adjutant had said. "What else can we do?"

Polzl looked at the English sergeant driving the truck, the armed captain sitting beside him. He wanted to trust them because they had been fighting soldiers like him, but the past two months of betrayal had made it impossible for him to trust anyone, and he doubted whether he ever could again. His fingers twisted restlessly first at one waxed wing of his long moustache then at the other. Even that reminded him of betrayal, the greatest of all. He had grown and groomed it in emulation of his emperor, his kaiser, and his kaiser had deserted him, deserted Germany, abdicated his throne. Polzl still found it hard to believe, but the continuing evidence of other desertions, other abdications in high places forced him to do so.

"We soldiers did not lose this war," he said out loud.

"That's a laugh," the sergeant said. Both he and the captain spoke perfect German.

"We were betrayed," Polzl told him. "Betrayed by our leaders."

"All right," Captain Barton said wearily. "If that's what you want to believe, you go ahead and believe it."

I always will, Polzl thought, always.

"Where are you taking me?" he asked again.

Barton studied his passenger's face in the driving mirror. With its jutting ears, its staring eyes and its ridiculous moustache it resembled, he thought, nothing so much as a clown. A sad serious clown. He wondered what possible use Brigadier Messiter could have for him. Perhaps pressure of work had finally driven the old boy round the bend, and he'd decided to leave the army and go into the circus business. Well, they were nearly there and soon he'd be rid of him. No harm in telling him now.

"Ypres," he said.

Polzl said nothing. He was remembering a damp cold night four years before when three and a half thousand men tramped westward through the mist toward that place, singing to keep step, to celebrate the victory which must lie ahead. Von Linder had been one of them, a lieutenant then, marching with them.

The shells had come without warning, howling and roaring out of the darkness, ripping apart the sable blanket of the night, and after them, the terrible iron greeting of the machine guns. They had fought for four days and at the end of that time more than half their number were dead or missing. Of these there was one in particular he could never forget, an Austrian corporal he'd known in childhood, a man from his own hometown, a man whose nerve had broken and who'd run, screaming with terror, from the guns. He could still see his livid face scoured with contemptible tears, still hear the echoes of his coward's voice, the sight and sound of defeat, forever indelible. Polzl had wanted to shoot him, destroy him before the germs of his betrayal could spread, but there had been no time. The man had fallen, still screaming, into the mud, his body screened by the stolidly advancing phalanx of his comrades. Perhaps he had drowned there, perhaps the enemy had succeeded where Polzl had failed. He had never seen the man again.

He had always prided himself on being one of the best runners in the regiment. But it wasn't anything so simple as just running. It was hard physical and mental endurance, a gamble against dangerous odds, a challenge, acceptable only because of his own constant belief that he must finally win, that his strength of will would continue to support him even when that of his body was exhausted. He had refused offers of promotion, preferring the solitude of his chosen task, conscious always of its responsibilities, its importance, and for much the same reasons had sought no popularity among his peers, made few friends, certainly none among the officers. But from a distance he had admired and respected the aristocratic von Linder. They had only once come into direct contact and that was when Polzl had delivered his report, complete with sketches, on the wild weird black-clad creatures he'd seen more than once in the lonely nights of No Man's Land. Von Linder hadn't laughed but had forwarded it intact to brigade HQ who had promptly dismissed it as rubbish and decreed that it must never be referred to or discussed at any future time. Von Linder had told him of their verdict, adding with amusement that only he, the officer, could be held responsible. Mere NCOs were never personally identified in dispatches to such high authorities, and as often as not, with fresh recruits constantly filling the gaps left by the dead, even their own officers had difficulty in remembering their names. Polzl had no doubt at all that after such a long lapse of time, the major would certainly be unable to remember his. That must have been why the British had insisted on taking his photograph, as a means of identification. He had never seen von Linder again after that day but felt relieved that he was still alive. People like him would be needed to rebuild Germany. Remembering their last meeting, Polzl suddenly realized that there could only be one reason for the major wishing to see him so urgently. He was glad he'd brought his sketchbook with him in his pack.

"Ypres," the captain said again. "D'you know where that is?"

Polzl didn't hear the question. His thoughts had leapt ahead to another night, barely three months ago, on a hill to the south of that same town. He heard again the drumfire of enemy gas shells, felt once more the searing burn in his eyes, the pain that had blinded him for long enough to end his war so near to where it had begun. The unconquerable place called Ypres.

"The name obviously means nothing to him," Captain Barton told his sergeant in English.

"This was a *town?*" Harvey James asked in shocked wonder as we drove into the ruins of Ypres. Only the scarred tower of the Cloth

Hall remained defiantly erect like the still visible mainmast of some great ship sunk beneath rolling waves of broken masonry, unidentifiable rubble.

Our billets were to be two miles closer to the Stroombeek Valley in the village of St.-Julien, where miraculously a few stone buildings still stood, but the Menin gate at Ypres was our rendezvous point with the men who were escorting von Linder's corporal. The brigadier would have commended their promptitude. They had arrived, Captain Barton told me after we had established each other's identities, exactly half an hour earlier. While waiting for us, he said, his passenger had passed the time standing on the shattered ramparts, a pencil and sketchbook in his hands, staring first at the devastated city and then out across the wilderness of what had been the salient.

"Some kind of war artist, is he? Gloomy sort of character, hardly says a word. What d'you want him for? Designing tombstones?"

"Something like that," I said.

The captain shrugged, climbed back into his truck.

"Rather you than me, colonel," he called as he drove off.

I watched Polzl walk stiffly up to von Linder, salute, present him with the sketchbook. For a meeting between two old comrades in arms, the occasion seemed singularly lacking in warmth.

"Germans," Barnes said. "No human emotion permitted between officers and other ranks."

"They'll be crying into each other's beer as soon as they're on their own," said Meadows.

It began to rain and only stopped after we'd reached our billets at St.-Julien. They consisted of the remaining half of a shell-blasted cottage and a small cattle shed a few yards away. We parked the lorries between them, unloaded guns, ammunition, binoculars, tinned food, water, sleeping bags. Barnes preempted any awkward decision on my part about sleeping arrangements by insisting that he and his fellow NCOs should occupy the shed. "You too, mate, if you want," he said to Polzl and waited while Askew translated.

"He says he'll sleep in the open," Askew said.

Barnes shrugged. "Hope it keeps fine for you," he said.

It was only after I and the other officers had installed ourselves on the ground floor of the cottage that I realized there was a large hole in the roof. I made a mental note to check closely on any further rank-inspired generosity from Fred Barnes and went out with Meadows to take the first watch. Baudroie and Askew would relieve us at midnight until three and then von Linder and Harvey James would take over until dawn.

"Guess I'll doss down in the lorry till I'm wanted," Harvey said. "Keep an eye on my stuff." He too had seen the hole in the roof.

"It looks like the surface of the moon after someone's used it for target practice," Meadows said as we swept the bleak horizon with our binoculars.

It looks like hell, I thought, after even the devil has deserted it. But somewhere in the stillness of that pitted earth, somewhere beneath the maimed leafless trees, the jagged scars of old trenches, the gaping craters, the hardening mud, I knew that devils of a kind still lurked. The search for them was to begin an hour after first light.

We handed over to Baudroie and Askew and stumbled back toward the cottage. I noticed Polzl lying in his sleeping bag beside James's lorry. His eyes were open and he was staring up at it. He didn't turn his head as we passed. Von Linder was waiting for me outside the cottage, a torch in one hand, something that looked like a child's exercise book in the other. "I want you to see this," he said and opened the book to show me the drawings Polzl had made.

"The first is a view of Ypres," he said and shone his torch onto it. No ruins, no rubble, but around the tower of the Cloth Hall the outline of a new city had arisen, simply but incisively drawn in thin firm pencil strokes.

"You didn't tell me he was an architect," I said.

Von Linder smiled. "He'd like to be. That one is imagination. The rest are not."

I turned to the next page. It was divided into three sections, each containing a circled position in or near the Stroombeek Valley. Penciled lines indicated their bearings and distances from the center and either wing of the Passchendaele ridge. I stared at them in amazement.

"Are these supposed to be accurate?"

Von Linder shrugged. "Polzl says so. They're copies of the drawings he made at the time. Let's hope his memory's a whole lot better than mine."

I looked at the sketches again.

"The places where he saw them," von Linder said.

I shivered. One of them, I thought, might be where I had lain that night waiting for the black claws to rip my body.

Von Linder switched off his torch.

"Now you know why I had to find him," he said.

I looked over toward the lorries. Polzl had turned his head, was watching us. He asked a question in German, and when von Linder had answered, turned away again.

"He wanted to know why we weren't starting the hunt. I told him to get some sleep first. Useless. I don't think that man ever sleeps."

It was a long time before I could sleep either, and when I did, it was to dream once more the nightmare of the men of Golgotha. I forced myself awake as Harvey James came into the cottage.

"Nix," he said. "Nothing to report. Not a damn thing to be seen. Maybe they're all dead. What's for breakfast?"

But they had seen us. The Priest had. He'd made it his invariable rule never to look for food himself on the surface, and Shaw, understanding his reasons, had not pressed him. But now that there was only fresh water to be found up there, he was always the first to volunteer. He knew when it had been raining because the moisture would seep down, threatening the structure of the walls, bringing its own smell, mephitic but more tolerable than the prevailing one of decay, the stench of death. He knew it had rained the day before, and that was why he was elbowing his way forward on his stomach, pulling a dixie can behind him, toward the nearest clay-based pool when he saw a light. He couldn't know that it came from von Linder's torch but he did know that it had not been there before. He lay very still, his body wedged into the drying mud, the wooden crucifix pressing against his chest. After a few moments the light disappeared, but he remained motionless, straining his eyes toward the place where it had been, and when they had again become accustomed to the darkness, he thought he could see two large objects between the ruined cottage and the cattle shed which also had never been there before. He squirmed round, careful not to raise even his head and was just in time to prevent three others of his flock, each with another dixie can, from appearing above the surface. He said nothing to them as they climbed and slithered downward. He was waiting until he was alone with the other leaders in the privacy of their cavern behind the sacking. Only then would it be safe to speak.

All three listened in silence to what he had to tell them. Then the Marksman wanted to know what kind of light he had seen. A fire? An explosion? Just a light, the Priest said. Shaw didn't seem interested in the light, only in the objects between the ruins, their shapes, their sizes. The Priest did his best to describe them and after a long silence a word from the past surfaced in Shaw's mind.

"Lorries," he said, and his teeth were suddenly bared as he glared at the others. Then he swept the sacking aside and ran from the cavern. The Marksman hurried after him and then, more slowly, the Shouter. The Priest knew where they were going. To the cave whose entrance was blocked by the side armor of the tank. They were going to fetch the guns. He had always known they had plans for what action to take if they ever felt themselves threatened from the world above, but they had kept them secret from him. Nevertheless, the Priest had guessed what they were and had those of his own, equally secret, shared only with the blind boy. He took an old square of thick cardboard from between the two strips of waterproof canvas on which he slept, satisfied himself that the words he had written on it were still visible, then called for the Acolyte who, he knew, would be waiting on the other side of the curtain. He read the words to the boy once more and asked if he remembered what he must do. The boy nodded, an eager smile lighting up his young blind face, and the Priest gave the cardboard square into his hands and told him to keep it hidden until the time came. The boy took the cardboard outside the cavern and lay down on it, covering it with his body. When he had gone, the Priest lifted the cross on the end of its leather thong and held it in front of his eyes. He had been praying for quite a time before he remembered that he'd left his dixie can up there beside the clay pool. There was no chance of retrieving it now, and in any case, he told himself, one more rusting object among the thousands which already littered the torn earth could be of no possible significance to anyone. He put it from his mind and returned to the more important matter of his conversation with God.

"It was agreed that we should go in peace," he told Him. "O blessed Savior, do not forsake us Thy servants in our hour of need."

CHAPTER 14

I ordered the lorries to be driven as close as possible to the first of
the positions given in Polzl's sketches.

My plan was to make a series of square searches looking for any
particularly marked declivity in the churned-up surface which
might lead down to further hidden tunnels, subterranean passages.

Von Linder trudged slowly at my side, slipping and staggering
through the silent debris of war, the broken ground itself, its arid
harvest of old steel helmets, twisted pieces of equipment, human
bones, often skulls. I did not need to see his face to know what was
in his mind. Our thoughts must be, could only be, identical. For
this torn and ravaged useless strip of earth, numberless thousands
had died. Into this small black square on the crazed checkerboard
of the generals and the politicians, unnamed legions had been
thrown to clash and be no more.

"Here!" Meadows shouted. "Over here!"

It was not one crater, but at least three or four joined together
to form a deep pit. Polzl stood on its lip, staring around him, taking
bearings, measuring distances. He nodded at von Linder as we
approached, not smiling, simply recording the accuracy of his
memory.

Askew, Meadows and Selfridge, it had been agreed, were to
remain permanently on the surface. Their special functions of
interpreter, arresting officer and doctor could best be performed
there whenever anyone requiring one or all of their services was

either flushed out and driven upward or pulled back to safety. Besides, they were needed to haul on the ropes which each of us would tie round our waists before beginning our descent. Harvey James was to wait with them, ready to bring down his gas containers should they be needed. No particular role had been foreseen for Polzl beyond the very important one of guiding us to our target. I asked von Linder to tell him to stay with James, help him with his heavy equipment. Polzl gave his customary expressionless nod. That left six of us. Barnes, the other two NCOs, Baudroie, von Linder and myself. We were to operate in two groups of three each. The first trio—in this case Barnes, von Linder and myself—would signal if they discovered any further possible means of descent leading on down from the original excavation. The second trio would then join and pass them, going even deeper while the first covered them as best they could with their automatic weapons and revolvers. The process would then be repeated in reverse order at a lower level and thus we would proceed in stages, one group always protected by the other a few feet above it. That was the theory. It had yet to be tried out in practice. No one knew how far down we'd have to go nor indeed what we might find when we got there. Hardly, as the brigadier had said, a picnic. I slithered down into the big crater followed by von Linder and Fred Barnes. He carried a miner's pick and a geophone apparatus slung round his neck. We all carried side arms.

For fully twenty minutes we crawled around its slimy base, von Linder and I scraping at the mud with our entrenching tools, our gloved hands feeling for anything which might conceal a hidden entrance, any man-made hole, even the smallest crack which could act as some sort of air duct. Barnes tapped assiduously with his pick, listened on his geophone. We found a splintered pelvis, the remains of what had been a leg, nothing more. No concealed apertures, no fissures, no sounds, Barnes reported, except for the scurrying feet and squeaking cries of rats. The crater was simply a crater. I signaled to the men waiting above us, and they helped to pull us up, our feet scrabbling and squelching against its dripping walls.

As we were cleaning off the mud, Polzl, his sketchbook open in his hands, came over to von Linder and spoke briefly.

"He says they must have closed it off," von Linder told me and smiled quickly when he saw my expression.

"I know how you feel," he said. "You'd like to stuff his damn sketchbook down his throat. But why not try the next one instead?"

I wished that Colonel Charles had taken bearings to pinpoint exactly where he'd put his package of untouched food but he hadn't.

So, *faute de mieux*, we tried the next position on Polzl's plans, a shallow ditch which crumbled under Barnes's pick to reveal what must once have been someone's dugout. Sodden bits of paper, a broken brandy bottle still lay on its floor.

"Looks as if we're getting somewhere," I called to the impatient group waiting above.

But we weren't. A further lengthy and minute examination proved beyond doubt that the dugout, like the crater before it, led nowhere.

I climbed out, von Linder's eager hand yanking me up the last foot to the surface.

"Look," he said. "Look over there."

I looked. Polzl was standing alone a few hundred yards away, staring toward the ridge of Passchendaele, absolutely motionless as though in a trance. Then he suddenly jerked round, pointed with the sketchbook toward his right.

"Third time lucky, maybe?" von Linder said.

I had no better suggestions to offer.

"All right," I said. "We'll try it."

We clambered back into the lorries. Translated by Askew, Polzl told the driver of the leading one the precise direction in which to go.

"If he's wrong this time," I said to Meadows, "you can arrest him and send him back to Germany."

"Fine by me," Meadows grunted. "Can't stand waxed moustaches."

We stopped on a piece of raised ground, its surface drier and firmer than the churned-up morass surrounding it. Once it must have been covered by a small thicket of trees but none remained now, only the jagged outlines of their shattered stumps. Two big craters, each about twenty feet deep, lay side by side, only a few yards separating their edges. Baudroie was the first man out of the lorries, stumbling eagerly over the broken ground like a ferret looking for rabbit holes. He suddenly bent down, picked up something, turned with it in his hands, started yelling excitedly.

"He's found an old dixie can," reported Askew. "He keeps saying it's French."

"There *were* other Frenchmen in this war," Harvey James said mildly. "Or didn't anyone tell him?"

"Perhaps he wants to take it back to the Louvre," said Selfridge.

Baudroie ran up to me, waved the can in my face.

"*Cette fois, c'est moi,*" he shouted.

"He means it's his turn to go down first," Askew said unnecessarily. I looked at von Linder. He shrugged. Behind him, Polzl was nodding.

"Fair's fair," Barnes said. "We've had first crack twice."

He was still scraping mud out of his ears.

Baudroie was already knotting a safety line round his waist, peering into the nearest crater.

"Tell him," I said to Askew, "to be very careful. If he finds anything, he's to report it and wait until we've joined him."

Baudroie was gesticulating and yelling at the other two NCOs to follow him. "And bloody well remind him that I'm in charge of this operation," I said angrily. "If he finds another Frenchman down there, he doesn't murder him. He tells him he's under arrest and sends him up to us."

Askew translated rapidly and loudly. Baudroie, already halfway down the crater, didn't even look up.

"*C'est un ordre!*" I shouted in my best French.

"*Merde!*" replied Lieutenant Baudroie in his.

I watched as the NCOs joined him, waited for several minutes while the three of them crawled around the crater's base. Then Baudroie gave a sudden whoop of triumph and I felt his safety line jerk in my hands as he disappeared literally into the earth.

"Stay where you are!" I yelled at the NCOs, but I was too late. Both had followed him and the second had drawn his revolver.

It had been Shaw's idea to carve small level platforms into the sides of the two exit shafts very close to their highest points, just a couple of feet below the twin slabs of metal which could be lifted aside to give access to one or other of the craters above them. Easy to get at temporary storage places for food rations or anything else found on the surface, he'd told the Priest. Faced now with the need to put one to its real use, he hadn't known which to choose, that in the right-hand shaft or the left. But he trusted St. Christopher, and the saint had always dangled from his right wrist. So he chose the right-hand platform. He squatted there now behind his machine gun, the Marksman close beside him cradling a rifle. They had been waiting there for several hours before Baudroie discovered the metal slab and flung it aside. Shaw fired a burst directly at him, driving his split torso back into the man following him. This man, too, died instantly from the same burst and the two mingled, mangled bodies hid for an instant that of the third behind them. In that instant Shaw took his finger from the trigger and the third man fired his revolver. The Marksman shot him through the heart before he could fire again, but not before Shaw had slumped forward across his gun, blood pouring from a wound in his head.

The roar of the guns echoed like distant thunder into the depths below, and hearing it, the Priest placed his hand on the Acolyte's head, at once a blessing and a signal. The time had come.

Inside his brain the boy heard the whisper of the Priest's voice describing to him the words he had written, telling him of the message he was to carry. "We are your brothers. We mean you no harm. We shall go with you in peace."

He needed no gift of sight to find his way to the surface. He had followed the Priest there more often than he could remember. The piece of cardboard concealed beneath the rags which hung from his shoulders, he began to climb quickly up the left-hand shaft. His heart was full of gratitude to the Priest for all his kindness, his trust. Now at last he could repay them.

I heard the firing, saw from above the three shattered bodies spew backward into the pit of the crater, the sucking mud close sickeningly over their dead faces. It was all over in less than fifteen seconds. My entire group stood still as statues, frozen into shocked immobility. "Grenades!" I yelled, and von Linder was the first to move, hurling his a split second before my own into the hole through which Baudroie had plunged to his death.

The Marksman heard the explosion above him, felt chunks of earth crash around and onto him as he slithered and scrambled down the shaft, one hand supporting Shaw's heavy body, the other grasping his machine gun.

The Acolyte continued his climb up the other shaft, the piece of cardboard no longer hidden but clutched in his hands ready to show to those who would be waiting for him on the surface. He was nearing it now.

The others were waiting for the Marksman at the bottom, rows of scared faces, a babble of screamed unintelligible questions. The Shouter moved rapidly among them, raising his arms for silence, trying to calm them. He was also ensuring that only those still capable of using them had been given guns and ammunition. There were sufficient for no more than one man in ten. The Priest thrust his way through the throng, gently lifted Shaw in his arms. He could feel the beating of his heart, knew he was still alive.

"Listen," the Priest shouted. "Listen to me." The noise subsided.

"Tell them you have weapons," the Priest said, "but do not use them unless they use theirs first."

He repeated the words in other languages, ignoring the Marksman's harsh laugh, the metallic rattle as he loaded a fresh belt into Shaw's machine gun.

The gas cylinders had been brought from the lorries. Harvey James had one strapped to his chest. He, von Linder and Barnes were going down with me. Askew as well this time. We all wore respirators.

"Gargoyles," I heard Selfridge muttering. "Gargoyles from outer space." Two spare cylinders lay on the ground in front of him.

I was about to slide over the rim of the crater where Baudroie had died when I heard Polzl's excited shout and then Meadows's sharp command.

"Get back, you!"

Someone had appeared in the bowl of the other crater holding in front of him an object which looked like a protective shield.

Meadows thrust Polzl aside and shot the Acolyte before he could take another step upward. His body spun round and the thing he was holding fell from his hands, disappeared into the hole from which he had emerged.

I ripped off my respirator, stumbled across to Meadows. His revolver was still trained on the prone body while Selfridge knelt to examine it.

"Only winged in the shoulder," he said. "Unconscious but still alive." He turned it over and I heard the surprise in his voice.

"He's just a kid—looks about eighteen."

"Get on with your bloody job," I said angrily. "Take him to the lorry, bring him round. I want an accurate description of every damn thing there is down there."

Selfridge looked up at me. His face was shocked, his head shaking in disbelief and for a moment I thought he'd made a mistake and the boy was dead.

"He's blind," Selfridge said.

The Priest had described to them all the piece of cardboard, the words of the message. Whoever was waiting up there would understand. There was nothing to fear. The strangers would come to them now as friends, not enemies. They would come in peace. The Marksman had snarled and pointed at Shaw still cradled in the Priest's arms while the Shouter tried to stem the blood which seeped more slowly now from his forehead.

Grouped between them, the rest had waited, looking from one to the other, unsure of what they should do, who they should follow. None had ever known their leaders to disagree before. That was why they had remained leaders.

The Shouter, as bewildered as any, had found himself praying silently. He was praying for the life of his friend Shaw, for the Acolyte on his important mission, for the Priest to be right. Jumbled prayers, confused. He wasn't sure to whom he made them, only that an answer must surely be given, a word, a sign.

The sign came first, like a spent leaf, like a stricken bird, fluttering down the left-hand shaft above them, turning over and over, twisting this way and that in the faint air currents as though desperately seeking to escape the agony of its death throes. It fell finally at the Shouter's feet and lay still, a piece of cardboard bearing a message of hope, now hopeless. They all stared at it in silence, no one moving. Then the Marksman gave a great roar of anger and stepped forward into the center of the crowd, the machine gun raised high above his head.

The Priest looked down at Shaw. He knew that he was not yet dead and could not decide whether he was glad or sorry, but he knew also what he had to do and so he carried him away. The Marksman signaled to the rest to take up positions around the walls. They obeyed him immediately and without questions. They had, once more, a leader. Only the Shouter hesitated. Shaw was his friend. He wished to be with him when he died, perhaps to die with him, so he made his decision, picked up the piece of cardboard, turned and followed the Priest. He was no longer present with the rest to hear the word which followed the sign.

It came from above in a rushing roar and some of those who heard believed it to be the voice of God or perhaps Satan and threw themselves to the ground, their faces pressed to the earth in terror.

It was neither. It was Major Askew bellowing through a megaphone, warning in one language after another that all must abandon whatever weapons they had, come up through the shaft one by one, and surrender. If the first of them had not appeared within two minutes, poison gas would be used to destroy them all.

He was still speaking when the Marksman climbed up the first few feet of the shaft with his machine gun, took careful aim, and fired a long burst.

I was aware of the megaphone flying past my face like a piece of paper caught in a sudden upward draft and then something hard, metallic, striking me in the stomach, winding me. Instinctively I grabbed at it and realized with horror that I was clutching Askew's black-gloved false hand, separated now from the rest of him which was falling, falling, bumping crazily against the walls of the shaft.

The world around me exploded in a terrifying blast of sound as Barnes and von Linder fired downward on either side.

"Gas!" I yelled at Harvey James. "Use the gas!"

He grabbed the carrying handle of the cylinder with his left hand, aimed it, and pressed the firing knob with his right. The gas spurted downward, a dragon's green breath, lethal.

The others stopped firing. No sound came from below. The earth walls of the shaft had been strengthened with strips of duckboard, pieces of metal. Rough uneven steps had been cut into them. Slowly, carefully, we began our descent through the swirling clouds of green vapor, the beams of the torches transforming it into an ever shifting kaleidoscope, iridescent, multicolored, an obscene bejewelled billowing curtain of death.

My limp was no handicap. We stopped every few feet to check each crevice in the walls of the shaft, no matter how small. All were empty.

"Whatever's down there'll be dead," Harvey James said. "Nothing can live in this stuff." Filtered through the respirator his voice sounded hollow, unreal. We continued our descent through the gradually widening shaft until sixty feet down it suddenly emerged into a large roughly circular area littered with what looked like motionless bundles of rags. But they weren't rags. They were men, dead men, their lives sucked from their bodies by the green mist still hovering over them.

We were standing on the floor of hell.

They had to be examined, each and every one, just to make sure, and so we began our grisly inspection. While the others were still completing it, I left them and began exploring the extraordinary spider's web of low alleyways which radiated from that central area. I found no one, alive or dead. Obviously they had all congregated together at the foot of the two shafts waiting to drive us out by force, confident in their madness that they could do it. We had found Askew's battered body lying among theirs. The sane and the insane united by death.

I stumbled over a thick slab of armor plating, perhaps a part of some destroyed command post, possibly a tank. It lay at the entrance to one of the smaller caves, and I entered that as I had each one, the Colt ready in my hand. Like the rest it was empty. As I turned to leave, I heard the shots.

None of the three still in the central area had seen a head move on its outer perimeter, lift itself from the dark sea of heaped rags into the deadly green light. It was wearing an ancient gas mask, the primitive sort issued in 1914, a sacklike cowl for the face and shoulders, two round glass-covered holes for the eyes, a piece of rubber protruding obscenely beneath them from the position of the hidden mouth like some black and rotted tongue.

The Marksman had kept it for years, telling no one. It was a precaution, as were Shaw's platforms at the top of the shafts. He didn't enjoy the act of killing, had run away from those who wished to kill him. But now they had found him again and it was still necessary, if possible, to survive. Those who had sent him to war had taught him that long ago and it was the reason he'd chosen his way, not that of the Priest. His lungs were swelling, the pain threatening to burst them. He knew the old mask could not withstand the gas much longer, knew as he strained to lift the machine gun that this was his last chance to observe their other favorite maxim.

If it comes to it, they'd taught him, make sure you take one of them with you. Hot tears blinded him and the heavy barrel swayed as his finger pressed the trigger.

I shot him with the Colt but I think he was as good as dead before the bullet hit him.

Von Linder and Harvey James lay sprawled on the ground.

"Guess that'll teach me not to hard-sell the product," Harvey said hoarsely as I bent over him. "Salutary lesson for the confident scientist." He'd been hit in his right leg which had crumpled awkwardly beneath him. Von Linder was alive too.

"Flesh wound in the buttocks," Barnes reported and grinned at him. "Painful, sir, but not fatal."

"Better than the balls," von Linder said and managed to grin back. We cleared a space against one of the walls, made them as comfortable as possible. I told Barnes to go straight up and fetch Selfridge, cursing myself for my stupidity in not having brought him down with us in the first place.

He looked at me anxiously. "But what if . . . ?"

"Get him!" I shouted.

He ran to the foot of the shaft, kicking bundles aside as he went.

"You get on with your search," von Linder said. "We'll be all right here." He looked at the huddled rags, then quickly away again. "At least no one's going to interrupt our conversation."

I didn't want to leave them in that dreadful place.

"You won't need your respirator once you're a couple of yards clear of this morgue," Harvey James said. "It's localized and it won't spread. On that I *am* right."

"I'll stay," I said. "There's no one else down here."

It was then that I heard the singing.

CHAPTER 15

I took off the respirator as I passed the piece of armor plating and, crouching beneath the low roof, staggered round one corner and then another, came out into a long straight passage where I was able to stand upright. The singing was much louder now and I recognized a tune I'd known since childhood although I couldn't understand the words. It came from behind a sacking curtain blanking off the far end of the passage.

I walked slowly toward it, the revolver ready in my hand, the respirator swinging from my waist. When I was a yard away, the singing stopped. I took another step forward and ripped the sacking from its fastenings.

It was a large cavern with a curved roof like a sort of dome and in it I saw two men dressed like the others in rags. The nearest spun round to face me as he heard the sound of the curtain tearing. His hands were lifted to the level of his chest and between them he held a square piece of cardboard. Incongruously, on one filthy wrist he wore a watch.

"Don't move," I said. "Don't either of you move." The second man clutched a rust-pocked mug in one hand, a lump of rotting bread in the other. A wooden cross hung from his neck.

"English," he said. "You are English. I ask you to read our message." There was an accent but the words were clear, the voice, like his face, calm.

I looked at the capital letters painted on the piece of

cardboard: WE ARE YOUR BROTHERS. WE BRING YOU NO HARM. WE SHALL GO WITH YOU IN PEACE. The message was repeated in French and German.

"Out," I said, gesturing with the gun. "Both of you, *out!*"

The man with the cross moved to one side, looked down, and I saw for the first time a stretcher raised a foot from the ground resting on two blocks of wood. A third man lay on it, his eyes closed, a dark patch of dried blood on his forehead. The stubs of two candles flickered uncertainly, one at his feet, the other at his head.

"I am the Priest," said the man with the cross. "My friend Shaw is dying. The psalm has been sung. The Twenty-third Psalm. I am about to give Holy Communion."

The first man said something in German. His tone was urgent, charged with meaning.

"The Shouter wishes you to know that Shaw is his friend also. He loves him."

I looked at the Shouter, then back at the Priest. They're insane, I thought. Both of them are quite mad.

"We are not mad," the Priest said. "We are the leaders here. We counseled peace to our people."

"Your people are dead," I told him.

The Priest bowed his head. "I ask your permission to continue," he said.

I looked at the blood on the forehead of the man called Shaw. Was he the one who had killed Baudroie? The one who would have killed me had the Frenchman not insisted on taking my place?

"None are without sin," the Priest said, "but the greatest is to deny a state of grace to one of God's children at the end."

I hesitated. Where the hell was Barnes? Had he found Selfridge? Was he taking care of von Linder and Harvey James?

The Priest was actually smiling. "Shaw is an Englishman. That does not matter to me and certainly not to our Savior. But it might to you."

I lowered the gun, nodded at him. If it was going to happen at all, better that it should happen without witnesses. One of them might tell the brigadier. I quailed at the mere thought of his sarcasm. Communion in Golgotha.

"Make it quick," I said.

The Priest raised his right hand, made the sign of the cross. "*In nomine Patris, et Filii, et Spiritus Sancti. Amen.*"

The left hand had joined the right, palms together, fingertips pointing up toward the curving roof, the earth which entombed them, the freedom of the heavens above, the universal posture of prayer to God by any name.

"*Introibi ad altare Dei,*" the Priest said.

Deep in the Shouter's consciousness, his child's consciousness, the ancient words awoke a chord of memory and he spoke the response as he had already sung the psalm, in a strong clear voice.

"*Ad Deum qui laetificat juventutem meam.*"

It was incredible, but it was true. Sixty feet beneath the earth's surface, two men whom I had supposed to be mad, whom I had been sent to arrest as traitors to their countries, were praying together in Latin for the soul of their friend. Two men of Golgotha seeking God's mercy for a third. And, in spite of myself, I felt moved, involved, a part of what was happening.

"*Judica me, Deus . . .*"

I heard a step behind me and turned, hoping to see Barnes. The son of a faith healer might understand.

It wasn't Barnes. It was Corporal Polzl, and he was carrying one of the spare gas cylinders, a respirator dangling from his neck.

"What the hell are you doing here?" I said angrily. "Your orders were to stay on the surface." I realized as I spoke that I was whispering and that he wouldn't understand anyway.

"I brought this for you," he said in German and indicated the cylinder. I seized the square of cardboard, thrust it in his face, pointed at the German version of the message.

"Surrender has been accepted," I said in the same language. "There is no more danger." I had learned these two elementary but important phrases as a means of reassuring frightened prisoners at the front.

Polzl took no notice. He was staring fixedly at the Shouter, his bright blue eyes suddenly pale, cold as ice. Angry red blotches suffused his thin cheeks and his teeth were biting into his lower lip, drawing blood.

"*Quia tu es, Deus, fortitudo mea,*" the Shouter proclaimed, his voice echoing round the cavern. *God is my strength.*

"Lambach," Polzl said, spitting out the word as a snake spits venom. The Shouter's voice faltered as he turned and saw him.

I could not understand the meaning of the guttural screams of abuse with which Polzl lashed him, but I saw the fear in the

Shouter's eyes, heard the dying fall of his own voice as he stammered out the next words of the response, the last he ever spoke.

"*Quare me repulisti . . . ?*" Why hast Thou forsaken me?

The Priest had moved in front of the stretcher, taken the Shouter's left hand in his right. They stood facing Polzl's fury, linked together like two figures in a child's paper cutout, protecting the body of Shaw, his departing soul, from the profanity of the curses. Suddenly they stopped, and in the silence the Priest spoke quietly to me in English.

"They come from the same village in Austria. Lambach."

The curses had stopped because Polzl was pulling the respirator over his face, strapping it tight. Only his eyes were visible now, ice-cold yet white-hot behind the glass lenses, the devil's eyes. His fingers stabbed the firing knob of the cylinder and the green gas spewed out its stream of death.

I tried to knock the thing from his hands, crammed my own respirator against my face, rushed blindly toward the two men. But I was too late. They had crumpled to the ground, their hands still linked, and when I bent to lift the Priest, I could just hear his last choking gasp.

"*Mea culpa. Mea maxima culpa.*" His clouded eyes flickered from me to Polzl and he was freeing us from all blame, telling us that the fault was his, all his. Then, slowly, they closed.

There was a hollow rattling sound as Polzl kicked the Priest's cup contemptuously across the floor. I rammed my revolver into his ribs, forced him backward out of the cavern and, when we reached the far end of the high-ceilinged passage, dropped my respirator and tore his from his head.

I shall never forget his face. It was twitching with uncontrollable spasms, glowing, sweating, as though at the height of orgasm, a dark vision of satisfied sadism, malevolent, malignant, demonic. I was looking into the face of evil.

"Good," he said in German and glanced down at the gas cylinder cradled in his arms like a newly found child, one always to be remembered, cherished. "This is good."

I took a step back from him, the Colt steady in my hand, leveled straight at his heart and was conscious of a weird sensation that time had stopped, that he and I were locked together in a moment which possessed neither beginning nor end, that would last forever unless one of us was able to break it. "I'm going to kill you," I said.

He stood very still, his eyes staring deeply into mine. I saw them change color, felt their magnetism. He too was aware of the strange infinitude of the moment enclosing us, was compelling me not to be the one who shattered it. My finger was on the trigger. All I wanted to do, all I needed was to press it and the imprisoning walls of that moment would be demolished, his evil would die with him. But I could not. It was as though I were paralyzed, literally hypnotized.

He shook his head, not in mockery but with self-assurance, the knowledge of victory. Then he turned and walked away.

I've no idea how long I stood there. Perhaps minutes, perhaps only a few seconds. The next thing I remember was Barnes in front of me staring down at the Colt which I still held in the firing position. "The doctor's with them," he said quietly and put his hand on the barrel of the gun, gently pushing it to one side, taking it from me. "All under control now."

I didn't know how much he'd seen. I hoped he'd seen nothing.

"There's no one else down here," I heard myself say. "Let's get out." I didn't tell him or anyone else, then or later, how the Priest and the other two had died because it would have meant confessing, facing up to my own guilt in allowing Polzl to live, and that I could not bear to do. So I bent and followed the light of his torch through the low passages back toward the hideous bundles of rags, the remains of the men of Golgotha.

Carrying von Linder and Harvey James on flexible stretchers, we began our slow ascent to the surface. Polzl was the first to reach it. He was still holding the gas cylinder. I watched Meadows take it from him, put it in one of the lorries, saw Polzl bend over von Linder, speak to him. Von Linder looked toward me, didn't answer. Polzl shrugged, moved away.

"As soon as we get to Ypres," I told Meadows, "that man is to be sent straight back to Germany."

"It'll be a pleasure," Meadows said.

"When we'd got you up to the surface," I said, "Polzl spoke to you. What did he say?"

We were in one of the lorries on the way to Le Touquet. Bunks had been rigged along its sides for von Linder and Harvey James. Barnes was driving. The vehicle jerked on the uneven surface and von Linder winced with pain as he answered.

"You were right to get rid of him."

"I asked you what he said." I realized I was shouting.

Von Linder turned his head, looked me straight in the face. "He said he was glad we'd killed them all. He said it would be a stupid waste of time and money to keep people alive who were of no use to anyone."

"Is that all?"

"Isn't it enough?" He looked shocked, angry. I knew he was telling the truth.

"He sure was fascinated by the gas cylinders," Harvey James said. "He never stopped trying to ask me questions about how to work them. Selfridge said he grabbed one of the spares to take down to you. That right?"

"That's right," I said.

"Did you use it?"

I glanced quickly at Barnes. He kept his eyes firmly fixed on the road ahead.

"No," I said. "I didn't use it."

Meadows was driving the second lorry.

"All ready to detain a crowd of dangerous homicidal maniacs," he said, "and what do I get? Him!" He jerked his thumb derisively over his shoulder toward where the blind boy lay sleeping on a stretcher.

"He's English," Selfridge said.

Meadows looked surprised.

"How d'you know?"

"He muttered something in his sleep. I only got one word."

"What?"

"Mother," Selfridge said.

"Poor little bugger," said Meadows.

CHAPTER 16

The brigadier appointed me to this job because he couldn't imagine anyone else would be able to handle it with more resourcefulness and discretion," Katherine said. "Well, I'm about to prove him right. Anyone want to argue?"

She looked challengingly at the four of us sitting in her room off the side ward which housed von Linder, Harvey James, and the blind boy.

"It's a bit unethical, isn't it?" Selfridge said. "I mean, medically speaking."

"Ethics," Katherine said scornfully and her eyes flashed. "When you've been a doctor a bit longer, doctor, you'll realize that there's more to it than taking care not to rape your lady patients, etcetera."

"If I had you as my nurse, Mrs. Garrard, I doubt if I'd even *notice* any lady patients, et cetera," Selfridge said.

A gallant enough answer, I thought, even though a bit out of his usual character. But then I was sure that he, like all of us, had been deeply affected by what she'd told us about the blind boy.

She had sat at his bedside for the greater part of two days and nights telling him he was safely among friends, encouraging him to talk. Toward the first evening he'd put out his hand and touched hers and, after she'd held it for a few moments, had started speaking and apart from intervals for sleep had hardly stopped since. He spoke, she said, in a matter-of-fact voice without self-pity, telling her of that other hand which had come from nowhere into his world of blackness, guided him away from the sound of invisible guns into a place of quiet and safety. The hand of the Priest, whose Acolyte he had become.

He actually laughed when he told her that he was the only one in that place who had no cause to complain of the darkness.

And then he'd gone on to decribe in detail the Priest and Shaw, the Marksman and the Shouter. Denied sight, his hearing had become more acute and he'd overheard many of their conversations, their arguments, their decisions, the lies and evasions they had practiced on each other. (I've used much of what he said to Katherine in this narrative.) He liked all the four leaders and many of the rest, but the Priest he loved. He was his mother and his father, his god.

A god, I thought, destroyed by a devil.

Katherine had asked him if he remembered his real parents.

"Oh yes," he'd said. "Mum didn't want me to volunteer, but Dad said I must. Lie to them about your age, son. Go and fight for king and country. I was sixteen but I told them I was nineteen and they believed me. Wasn't I silly? Dad was real proud."

"Stupid bloody sod," Barnes had said when Katherine reported this part of their conversation.

"So we're all of us agreed then, aren't we?" she asked in conclusion. "We simply tell everyone he was brought here by a French family who'd been looking after him."

"*We're* all agreed, Katherine," Roy Meadows said. "*You* tell the brigadier."

She didn't. She told Colonel Charles instead who made immediate arrangements for the boy to be enrolled at St.-Dunstan's. He didn't stay there long because, they said, he didn't need to.

"Quite amazing progress," Charles said to Katherine at the farewell dinner the brigadier had insisted on giving for all of us in the room at Carlton House Terrace, after he'd read my full report on the Golgotha Gamble. Full, that is, except for any reference to the Priest's death, my shame in allowing it. "If you hadn't assured me to the contrary, I'd swear that lad had been living in some place where he'd learned to feel his way around by touch alone," Charles said. "Some deep dark place."

The brigadier was sitting between them at the head of the table.

"Like Golgotha, for instance, Anthony?" he asked cheerfully.

Colonel Charles frowned.

"Appalling bad taste, that, Henry."

The brigadier looked immediately contrite.

"Quite so. I do apologize." He smiled across at me—the trusting model. "Besides, if that had been the case, you'd have said so in your report, wouldn't you, Garrard?"

I assured him that I would.

He nodded gravely. "As the guardian of many secrets," he said, "I've always prided myself on the ability to distinguish quickly between the true and the false. My dear friend Anthony Charles has persuaded, has taught me to see less precipitately. Some warm-hearted falsehoods are kinder, more worthy than a thousand cold-blooded truths."

The collective sigh of relief around the table was embarrassingly audible. We knew that they knew. The guardian of secrets had added one more to his treasury and the Acolyte was safe.

I never saw him again. Perhaps he's alive somewhere today. They say that blind people tend to live well into old age and he was, after all, only eighteen at the time.

But he was spoken of again that night.

"That day we found him," Meadows said, "after I'd winged him. Polzl wanted us to kill him right away."

We were back in our apartment, an unofficial nightcap after the headmaster's official end-of-term dinner.

"I didn't say so then," Selfridge said, "but I'd call that man a psychotic."

"I'd call him a shit," Harvey James said without hesitation. "No offense, Max." I looked at von Linder. He was leaving for Germany the next day and had already told me of his anxiety as to what conditions and states of mind he might find there.

"We're a proud people," he'd said. "Versailles has destroyed our pride, left nothing but a vacuum. One must be restored, the other filled. Difficult and dangerous in the wrong hands." He'd meant the Reds, of course, the new central council. Most Germans were incapable of looking much further ahead in those days. But some glimpsed a different more distant future. A few thought of nothing else.

"Polzl," Max said now. "Strange that I couldn't remember a name like that."

"I'd forget it again, sir, if I was you," Barnes said. "That man's got a curse on him."

I looked at him sharply. "Is that a personal observation or are you being psychic, Fred?"

"Bit of both," Barnes said.

Meadows tapped his finger against von Linder's chest. "Gypsy's warning," he said. "Forewarned is forearmed."

Selfridge was the first to leave. He had to be up early in the morning to discuss the lease of rooms in Harley Street.

"I look forward to seeing any of you whenever you feel the need," he said, "but take heed, I shall not be cheap."

A careful man to the end.

Harvey James made no pretense of his eagerness to return to America. "Wilson's League of Nations is one thing," he said, "but a Republican President smart enough to realize the U.S.A.'s a good three thousand miles from Europe is better. We'll get one next time. You can bet on it. I'll keep you posted."

Fred Barnes had planned to catch the night train to Cornwall but in spite of several reminders from Katherine had decided to have a few more drinks and miss it. Meadows said he'd find him a bed at his barracks in Chelsea.

Max von Linder was the last to go.

"You'll keep in touch with us," I said. "Let us know how things are going?"

He promised he'd do that.

"You're good friends," he said warmly. "We all need them. Particularly us Germans."

I dreamed that night of the Priest's cavern, only it wasn't the cavern but a much larger room of the same shape and there was no sign of the Priest. There was no sacking curtain at the single exit either but in its place a great oak door bolted on the inside. The room was full of people, many of them children. Katherine was there with our own child, a boy. I couldn't see his face although everyone was looking at me, silently begging me to withdraw the bolts, open the door, let them out.

I understood that they were not frightened, that they all had confidence in me. I tried the bolts but could not move them, and when I looked round to admit failure, Katherine and the other grown-ups had disappeared and all the children had their backs to me and were kneeling as though in prayer. But they weren't praying. I heard the sound of their weeping and knew that I was unable to comfort them, that it was too late. Then cutting across their cries, I heard the rattle of a machine gun, the hiss of gas.

I woke trembling. A fat pigeon was keening on the windowsill and someone was using an electric drill in the road outside.

Katherine called from the kitchen. "Kettle's boiling over. Tea on the way."

She brought in the tray together with the morning paper. The *Stop Press* referred briefly to an accident on the Great Western Railway. Several passengers on the night train to Cornwall had been badly injured.

"Fred really is a psychic, you know," she said.

Our son George was born four months later, baptized by the same vicar who had married us in his lovely church of Minster. Fred Barnes was the principal godfather.

"May God grant this child a long, happy and peaceful life," the vicar said and dipped his fingers in the ancient font and made the sign of the cross on the baby's forehead. He cried as he felt the cold touch, and with a sudden chill of fear I remembered my dream.

It was a beautiful warm June day, and outside, the churchyard was bright with summer flowers. I looked at Barnes. He held himself ramrod straight, but he was shivering as though an icy blast of air had blown through the stone pillars of the church.

CHAPTER 17

From Max von Linder, June 2nd, 1920

. . . The mark continues to fall while new political parties continue to rise. They rant at each other, often come to blows, offer no satisfactory solutions and soon give place to others. General von Seeckt commands what remains of our army after Versailles, and he alone seems capable of maintaining some sort of stability, favoring neither the Left nor the Right, but simply discipline, order. (Those two old German gods, I can hear you saying!) But we are lucky to have him. He never served on the Western front—you may know he was chief of staff to Mackensen in the East before he went to the Balkans and Turkey—so perhaps he is untouched by the madness which marks so many of those who did. The latest group of fanatics claiming to save Germany was formed in Munich last February. They call themselves, believe it or not, the Nationalsozialistische Deutsche Arbeiter-Partei. You must tell Brigadier Messiter. I remember how much he enjoyed rolling lengthy German titles off his tongue. He would make this one sound like an aria from Wagner . . .

He did, relishing every syllable, beating time with his fingers on a black-covered folder between the shell cases. Unlike most of his collection, it was still fairly thin.

"I understand their principal aim is to abolish the terms of the Treaty of Versailles," he said. "I am also informed that they are known more colloquially as Nazis. An unpleasant-sounding name. Vulgar, don't you think?"

From Max von Linder, December 15th, 1923

. . . The Nazis staged a march through the streets of Munich last month. Apparently there were about three thousand of them. It was, I believe, a pathetic attempt to emulate Mussolini's so-called "march on Rome" last year. The police broke it up with machine guns and those responsible were arrested for high treason. The great tragedy is that von Ludendorff was among them. The old man must have taken leave of his senses (western front madness?).

I send you and Katherine every good wish for a very happy Christmas and a peaceful and prosperous 1924.

Yours as ever, Max

P.S. The papers anticipate that the leader of the march will be sentenced to at least five years in prison. Good.

"They let the bloody man out after nine months," the brigadier said almost a year later and thumped his fist down onto the black file. It was by this time considerably thicker.

"It seems he used this classic gestation period to produce his own sort of offspring. Some damn great book. One of my bright young men will have to translate it if it's ever published."

"What's his name?" I asked.

"The jailbird author? Hitler. Adolf Hitler."

He opened the file, took a photograph from the back, handed it to me.

"That's him. A bit like Charlie Chaplin don't you think?" The brilliantined hair had been carefully parted on the right-hand side and the winged waxed moustache reduced to a central black square, but the eyes, staring, hypnotic, were unmistakable. I was looking at the face of Corporal Polzl.

* * *

That Christmas of 1924, the sixth of peace, the fifth of my son's life, was marred by the first serious row Katherine and I had ever had.

"George was crying this afternoon, Adrian."

"I know."

"He told me he'd been asking you about the war and you lost your temper and shouted at him."

"Perfectly true."

"It's natural that he should be curious about it."

"It's even more natural that I should want to forget it."

I'd spent the day finishing off the decorations. Pieces of mistletoe hung all over the place. I was sitting beneath one of them now. Katherine came over and tried to kiss me, but I turned my head away.

"You don't understand," I said.

"Oh, yes, I do. I understand very well. Millions of people want to forget it. That doesn't mean they have to swear at their children on Christmas Eve. What's so different about you?"

Polzl, I thought, that's what different. But I hadn't been able to tell her at the time and I certainly couldn't now in that quiet Cornish drawing room with the softly lit crib of Bethlehem standing in front of the fireplace. I stared at it and saw instead his face.

"I really shouldn't drink any more if I were you," Katherine said.

"Well, you're not me, are you?"

She stood looking down at me for a moment then moved to the tree, switched off the string of multicolored lights.

"I used to think we were so close that we were almost the same person," she said gently. "Perhaps I was wrong."

I tried to get up from my chair, knocked over the glass of brandy.

"I'm going to bed now," she said.

I spent the night, unsleeping, in the spare room, telling myself it was because I didn't want to wake her.

In the morning, on Christmas Day, I wrote to Max von Linder. It was more than eighteen months before I received an answer.

Berlin
August 4th, 1926

. . . My sincere apologies for not writing sooner, but the house in Schleswig-Holstein has been sold and the new owners (a Jewish family) have apparently been on an extended trip abroad. Your letter was only forwarded to me a few weeks ago. I have been living in Berlin for two years now learning how to become a stockbroker. Even old soldiers must eat and I'm actually managing to make a reasonable living since the currency reforms have stabilized the mark.

. . . I find it hard to believe, Adrian, but I suppose it is just possible that you may be right.

The maiden name of Adolf Hitler's mother *was* Polzl, Klara Polzl. He refers to her in the first part of his book, *Mein Kampf.* (It was published a month ago and I have just obtained a copy.) She died in 1907 when he was eighteen and he was devoted to her. He could have been using her name as some sort of safety measure, a disguise, when he was engaged in his spying activities on Communist elements in the military immediately after the war— at the time, in fact, when he was sent to us at Stroombeek. I have tried to find the adjutant of my own regiment, but I've lost touch with old army friends. All that seems like another world now. Perhaps Hitler *was* his name when he was one of my soldiers. I have racked my brains to try and remember but I simply cannot—there were so many of them. And I can hardly approach him directly to ask now! He moves in higher, more rarefied circles—Ludendorff, Krupp, even President Hindenburg. . . . Do you realize it is exactly twelve years since the war began? Let us pray there is never another . . .

I hope you and Katherine are well and happy . . .

We were the first but, sadly, increasingly not the second. It was chiefly because of the boy, Katherine's protectiveness toward him, and to be honest, my jealousy of it. Not only that, his incessant interest in the war, his everlasting questions.

"He's only a kid with a kid's imagination," Katherine said. "I do think you might at least try not to criticize him every time he opens his mouth."

She began coming less frequently to London during the weeks, and often, pleading pressure of work, I didn't bother to go down to Cornwall at the end of them. I was by now a permanent member of the brigadier's staff.

"I don't seem to have seen much of your lady wife recently," he said, and, having avoided asking a question, waited patiently for an answer. It was a bank holiday weekend and I'd planned to be home for dinner on the Friday evening, the day before George's eleventh birthday.

"She prefers the country," I said.

"Ah yes. Like Anthony Charles. We've bought a house near Beaconsfield, you know. Eventually I shall retire there, but for the moment I make flying visits to tell him how to cook, and he tells me how I should be running this department. I've always felt that an ability to understand and share each other's problems is a distinct advantage in any close personal relationship."

Another unasked question, but if we were trading domestic secrets, there seemed little point in attempting to camouflage mine.

"We tell each other how to bring up our son," I said.

The brigadier raised a warning finger. "Beware of jealousy, Garrard. The would-I-were-in-that-cradle syndrome. Have you heard from our friend Max von Linder lately?"

"Not for some time."

"Do try to keep in touch," he said as he locked the black file away till the following Tuesday. "I am informed that the Nazis are confident of more than a hundred seats in the Reichstag at next September's elections. The bloody man is on his way. The future is dark. Each shred of light from whatever source is welcome."

When I arrived the house was empty. I read the note which Katherine had left. "We're having supper with Fred."

"He had a super chap staying with him," my son said when they returned. "He's something terribly important in the police now but he used to be in the army. He told me *lots* about the war. He really is super, isn't he, Mum?"

"I've always liked Roy Meadows," Katherine said.

She was very solicitous to me that evening, insisting on cooking a late meal of bacon and eggs. I heard her humming happily to herself in the kitchen. When we went upstairs, she told me she'd have to wake early to take George rabbit shooting with Barnes and Meadows.

"I'll sleep in the spare room," I said to save her having to make the suggestion. It had become an increasingly regular habit in any case.

George delayed opening his presents until they returned for lunch the next day. One was a small bronze cross, its arms bent back at right angles. "A very ancient symbol of good luck," Max von Linder's note said, "to bring you lots of it and my best wishes for your birthday . . ."

Katherine had given him a game called Western Front, a Flanders version of snakes and ladders. You threw dice and moved small effigies of British and German soldiers across a board marked with various hazards and encouragements such as "machine gun nest, retire three squares," "reinforcements, advance one." They played it together throughout the afternoon while my own offering of a cricket bat stood forgotten in a corner. George invariably chose to be the Germans and usually won.

"There's a boy from Germany at my school," he told us. "He says their army never really lost the war. They were betrayed by the people at home. Jews and people like that."

Katherine glanced nervously at me.

"I don't think that's quite true, dear."

"It's damned nonsense," I said. "Where does he get such rubbish?"

"From his father," George said and grinned at Katherine. "Some *like* telling their sons about the war."

I kept my temper.

"And who gave his father this information?"

"He read it in a very important book by someone who *knows*," George said and frowned in concentration, determined to get the name right. "Adolf Hitler."

I grabbed the playing board, slammed it shut, scattering tiny soldiers all over the floor. George yelled with fury and hurled the bronze swastika at me. It struck me on the forehead above the right eye. I lashed out blindly, hit him across the face with the flat of my hand.

"I hate you!" he screamed and I would have hit him again if Katherine hadn't moved quickly between us.

"You should be ashamed," she said, and, of course, I was. But not only because I'd clouted my own son. I had lived with a greater shame than that for a long time and I still did.

That night I dreamed I was in Golgotha once more, confronting Polzl outside the dead Priest's cavern, the Colt revolver in my hand. I fired it, but he didn't fall. Instead he became George, holding the crooked cross up to my eyes and laughing. I ran past him to try and escape, to reach the surface, the clean air, but one of the bundles of rags rose to its feet and raised its hand to stop me. It was Katherine.

In the morning I found Fred Barnes alone in the kitchen. "They've gone shooting again," he said. "I thought I'd come over and fix your breakfast."

I told him I was perfectly capable of managing it for myself.

"You look terrible," he said. "Had a pretty bad dream last night, didn't you?"

"Please Fred, none of your psychic stuff. Not now, I've got a headache."

He cut two pieces of bread, put them in the toaster.

"Look," he said. "I think you'd better tell Katherine before it's too late."

"Tell her what?"

"What happened at Stroombeek. Polzl."

The kettle gave a shrill whistle and he filled the teapot. "Lance the boil, Adrian. Get rid of the poison before it destroys you and your marriage. That's what it's doing. She can't stand much more."

I stared at him, trying to take it in. He must have known all the time, must have been close enough to hear, perhaps even to see how the Priest and the others had died.

"Why didn't you tell me you knew?" I said.

"I didn't. Not for sure. Not everything. Not till now."

He put the teapot and some milk onto a tray.

"I saw you and I saw Polzl. You were facing each other. Then he turned and walked past me with the gas cylinder in his hand. He was smiling. You just stood there holding the gun like you'd been turned to stone. I looked in the cavern and saw the bodies, the cross, the bit of cardboard with the words on it. Then I came back and took the Colt from you."

He lifted the pieces of toast, laid them carefully on a plate.

"Polzl had murdered them and you'd let him live. And you've never been able to forgive yourself. You still can't. That's it, isn't it?"

"I never shall," I said. "Never."

He added butter and marmalade to the tray, checked that everything was present and correct.

"I know. I took a close look at a picture of Hitler last night. No need for psychic stuff there. Remarkable likeness. Tell her, Adrian.

Tell her that's why you hit the boy. Tell her everything. She'll understand."

So, when we were alone that evening, I told her. About the deaths of the Priest and the Shouter, about how I'd allowed Polzl to live, about who he was now. Everything.

She said nothing for several minutes and then the words came slowly, each one a release from remembered pain.

"For years now I've never been able to feel we were really together, never felt at ease with you. There was always another presence there. Something coming between us, keeping us apart, separate. I felt I was the intruder, in the way, unwanted. All I could think of was to try and protect our son from it. From that evil presence."

"And now?" I said.

She put out her hand, held mine.

"It was as though I couldn't touch you, couldn't reach you," she said.

I waited till I felt the tension in her relax and then I put my arms around her and held her close.

Next morning while we were having breakfast in bed she suddenly started laughing.

"D'you know I was actually thinking of leaving you."

"For Roy Meadows?"

"Never mind," she said and laughed again. "Although if it had been, I think George would have approved the choice."

"Forewarned is forearmed," I said. "I'll shoot rabbits with him all day and then get down to Western Front." I managed to laugh too, but the realization that I might really have been so close to losing her was like a knife in my heart.

Before I left for London, she promised not to speak to anyone of what I'd told her, not even Fred who already knew, and I promised that the evil ghost had been laid, that I'd never think of it again. We were both lying, of course, although I didn't discover until much later that she'd already written to the brigadier. If any marriage is to endure, I suppose that all lovers must lie from time to time in order to protect the loved one.

"I have a very interesting and important job for you," Messiter said a few months later. "Liaising with our friends in far-flung places, collating facts, bringing them up to date. You'll be leaving in

December. Be away from Europe for at least three years, perhaps longer."

I started to protest but he interrupted me.

"It is still a very large empire, Garrard, and I don't want the job skimped. Besides there's America. I'd say six months there at least. Very important, America."

"I've a wife and son," I said. "They are much more important."

"Quite so. Just as it should be. I have therefore prevailed upon our financial watchdogs to allow them to accompany you. Peace of mind in personal matters leads to greater efficiency in professional ones, etcetera. They growled a bit but finally wagged their tails albeit with some reluctance."

"But George is going to public school."

He smiled. The roguish model.

"All the more necessary for him to be given a proper education at home. He can join you for the holidays."

During the next few years, whenever time allowed, George did just that in such places as Canberra, Auckland, Pretoria, Delhi, Singapore, Ottawa, Washington, and many more. The brigadier had been right. The job was important, worthwhile, and I like to believe that the direct contacts I made, the interchange of views and information, all bore some fruit later when it mattered most.

It was a very happy time, a sort of delayed honeymoon with, for me, the additional bonus of coming to know and love my son.

At the end of it I was due for three months' leave, and Harvey James invited us to spend the last of them at his house in Lake Forest near Chicago. Katherine was reluctant to accept at first and I guessed the reason.

"I won't talk about the last time we met," I said, "and I'm sure he won't want to either."

He didn't. Nearing sixty but not looking it, he was far too preoccupied with his work as a senior lecturer at his university. There was a bunch of real bright kids on campus, he told us, even the ones who were Democrats. He invited a colleague to dinner one night, a professor of physics who had left Munich a year before in order to become an American citizen.

"Germany's loss is our gain," Harvey said before he arrived. "The guy's brilliant. Adolf Hitler's not only a shit, he's crazy too."

If Katherine hadn't been there, I might have reminded him

that he'd used the same word to describe the same man before. A shit's a shit by any other name. Even Polzl.

But she was there so I changed the subject.

"I was one of the lucky ones," the physics professor said at dinner. "I had money so I was able to buy my way to freedom. But the others who are still there . . ." He paused, stared down at his plate, suddenly pushed it away from him. ". . . They'll starve in the camps. Unless they kill them first." He looked up at Harvey. "Hitler's executioners are using poison gas chambers now."

CHAPTER 18

I'm glad your long sojourn in foreign parts was successful from a personal as well as a professional viewpoint," the brigadier said. Another unasked question awaiting an answer. We were lunching at his club, a sort of reward after months of intensive study and analysis of the reports I'd brought back for him.

"It was," I said.

"I had anticipated no less."

He raised his glass, drank slowly, savoring the wine.

"To intuition," he said. "When correctly applied, the cornerstone of all intelligence work. Alas though, a quality remarkable only for its absence among our present political leaders. Their Pavlovian reactions to the alarming progress of Herr Schickelgruber makes the head-in-sand ostrich appear a veritable vigilante by comparison."

Since the death of Hindenburg, Hitler had become the sole ruler of the German people, combining the offices of Chancellor and President under a single new title: Führer.

"There is, I'm happy to state, one notable exception," Messiter said. "Like myself, one who enjoys the undoubted blessings of an American mother." His deliberate use of the misnomer favored by that exception and delivered with a similar amount of pronunciative relish confirmed my guess that they had been meeting fairly frequently of late.

"What are your intuitive feelings regarding Herr Schickel-gruber, Garrard?"

"Someone should have killed him a long time ago," I said.

A bishop, in full fig, passed us, glanced at me with apprehension.

"Good afternoon, Edward," the brigadier said cheerfully. "How goes the battle with Satan?"

The bishop gave a nervous smile, moved hurriedly away.

"Before he had the chance to kill so many others. Is that what you mean?"

The Priest and the Shouter had only been the beginning. I remembered how he'd cradled the gas cylinder in his arms. "Good," he'd said. "This is good."

I remembered the professor in Lake Forest.

"That's exactly what I mean," I said.

The brigadier refilled our glasses.

"I was most interested in the last communication you received from von Linder," he said.

I'd had no hesitation in showing him the letter. Max had written to say that he had joined the Nazi party. He'd also become the senior partner in his firm, a position previously held by an internationally respected Jewish banker.

. . . I felt despair when Hindenburg forced von Seeckt to resign, but now the bumbling old fool has gone too, and at last Germany has a real leader, a true sense of purpose, a new destiny. The Führer has many British friends and greatly admires your country. It is rumored that your future king plans to visit him soon. Why don't you and Katherine come to see our new Germany for yourselves? An even better idea—be my guests at the Olympic Games here in Berlin next August. It will be such a splendid occasion, a spectacle such as the world has never witnessed before. The great stadium is almost complete with seats for a hundred thousand spectators. It would give me so much pleasure if you were to be among them. The Führer himself will perform the opening ceremony . . .

"Have you accepted his invitation?" the brigadier asked.

"For myself. Not Katherine. School holidays."

"Ah yes. Quite so."

He took off his glasses, wiped their lenses carefully on a silk handkerchief. I could see dark circles under his eyes.

"You've never met Herr Hilter, I suppose?"

The direct question was like a physical shock. I could not have answered even had I wished to. The whole sedate room seemed to shake as though in the grip of a sudden storm, as though some dark force had taken possession of it. The triumphant demonic face swam in front of me. I saw again the contemptuous shake of his head as he turned to walk away from me, alive, unharmed.

"I have," Messiter was saying. "Von Papen gave a reception for him in Berlin. I stood in line and shook the monster by the hand."

He replaced the glasses.

"We're all to blame, Garrard," he said, "all of us who have recognized a poisonous plant and yet lacked the strength or the courage to cut it down." I stared at him. Had he guessed? Could his precious intuition have carried him that far? And if so was he condemning me or trying to offer comfort, an assuagement of guilt?

But the pebble glasses hid his eyes, his secret thoughts.

I puzzled over the answer to these questions for weeks, but it was only when Katherine asked me whether the brigadier had approved my decision to accept Max's invitation that the truth suddenly hit me. She must have repeated to Messiter everything that I'd told her about what had happened at Stroombeek. I didn't even pretend to be upset or angry. She had broken her promise but only in an attempt to help me. Nor did she try to deny it.

"He'd have sent you on that trip round the world in any case," she said. "He'd already planned it. But please don't tell him I've confessed. He'd be furious. How did you guess anyway?"

"Intuition," I said.

The brigadier was fifty-five years old and due to retire as head of the department at the end of the year. Naturally he'd seized on the opportunity to give a series of farewell dinners for all those who had worked with him.

"I'll start with your friends Barnes and Meadows," he said. "Yours will have to wait until after the Olympics. I take it you'll be going in a purely unofficial capacity, as a private individual?"

I assured him I would.

"I have to admit," he said reflectively, "that I shall find it hard to relinquish the reins. This work of mine is very near my heart. Almost an obsession one might say. But then we all have our obsessions, don't we?" He lifted the black file from his desk, held it for a moment, studied its blank cover with absolute concentration, set it down again.

"I shall be most interested to hear what you make of your visit to Berlin," he said.

It was a perfectly simple, seemingly straightforward remark, and yet he had obviously chosen the words with great deliberation. Knowing the complexity of his mind, I wondered if they were some sort of code, concealing another, more arcane message. A warning perhaps. An intuitive warning.

"Obsessions can be dangerous," he said quietly. "We should all remember that. But ignoring them might be considered dangerous too." A warning then but also perhaps a signal to act, a green light? Purely unofficial, of course.

"How about a spot of lunch?" he said.

"Be sure to give Max my love," Katherine said, "and you will promise to be careful, won't you?"

I kissed her, smiled. "I promise," I said.

One more lie. The tiny automatic was already packed in my suitcase, so small that it fitted neatly into an otherwise empty cigarette tin.

Max had reserved two of the best seats in the stadium. Three rows above the flower-strewn path the Führer would take on his progress to the supreme podium to light the Olympic Flame, declare the Games open.

"There will be doves," Max said, "white doves of peace. A hymn specially composed by Richard Strauss."

He had taken me on a tour of the spotless city the day before. "I'm so happy you're here to see it for yourself at last, Adrian. Not a sign of anti-Semitism. No dreadful posters of Jewish bloodsuckers. All that's just propaganda."

And so it seemed. There were no such posters. But I had noticed two young storm troopers tardily tearing down a proclamation nailed to the door of a jeweler's and looked up at the faded name of the proprietor above it. Rosenfeldt. Max had pointed quickly in the opposite direction, at the crowds already streaming toward the stadium a full twenty-four hours before the ceremonies were due to begin.

"All propaganda," he said again, "like that nonsense about concentration camps. See how happy they look, so well-behaved, so welcoming."

They did indeed. Germans, I thought, had always been good at obeying orders.

We had dined together at the Adlon, a table in a window recess, one of the best. It was hard to believe Max was seventeen years older than when I'd last seen him. In many ways he actually looked younger. The haunted look had disappeared, something which belonged to a distant past, forgotten. His eagerness, his high spirits, his confidence, all these belonged to the present, the even more exciting future. I gave him Katherine's messages, felt once more the full warmth of an affection which had never really cooled. It was a reunion of two old friends who'd been too long apart. Neither of us mentioned the Stroombeek valley and for the space of that happy meal I put aside all thought of what I must do the following day. A letter completely exonerating him from any knowledge, any form of complicity in it, was in my wallet next to my identity papers where they would be sure to find it quickly.

"To us," Max had said, raising his glass. "To our friendship."

"To the future," I'd replied. "To peace."

A roll of drums, a blast of trumpets, a sudden vibrating expectant silence engulfing the vast multitude, each head turning, every pair of eyes straining to watch for the approach of their Führer.

Then, as they saw him, the cheers which were so much more than cheers. A great swelling paean of orchestrated adoration, the voice of a nation welcoming and worshipping its new god, its savior, its Siegfried come again.

The automatic was in the right-hand pocket of my jacket, slim, light, causing no bulge. It could fire three bullets, but I prayed that one would be enough.

I could see him now, escorted by his personal SS bodyguards, flanked by the lesser princes of his kingdom. He walked as an emperor might, a little ahead of them all, head twisting from side to side, lips smiling beneath that ridiculous moustache, right hand raised again and again in proud salute, in lofty acknowledgement of his people's greeting. Even after seventeen years I had no doubts.

None at all. The last time I had seen his face was in the valley of Stroombeek, the place of Golgotha.

I put my hand in the pocket of my coat, gripped the butt of the automatic, felt for the handkerchief which was to conceal it.

He stopped ten yards away, patted the head of a child while his cohorts smiled their approval and innumerable cameras recorded the moment for history.

"The Führer asked especially for him to be presented," Max said reverently. "The boy is blind."

I stared at him, astonished, appalled.

"My God!" I said. "Don't you remember?" but my voice was drowned in a mighty roar of acclamation as the Führer moved on, as Polzl moved closer toward me.

One bullet was all that was necessary for expiation, to do that which I had left undone for so long.

He was almost level with me now. Hiding it under the handkerchief, I took the little gun out of my pocket. And then as though to make my task easier, as though offering himself for execution, he turned his head and looked directly at me. My finger on the trigger, I took careful aim between his eyes.

(The Narrative, as such, stopped here. The last few pages consisted of numbered extracts from various memoranda and one newspaper article. Then a final coda written in my grandfather's own hand.)

1. Chief Superintendent Meadows to Brigadier Messiter
August 27th, 1936

Ex-sergeant Barnes and myself carried out your confidential instructions given to us at dinner on August 2nd. We both got a close look at Herr Hitler. Colonel Garrard was correct. There is no doubt in my mind that the Führer and Corporal Polzl are one and the same man. Barnes confirms this. Material recovered from Colonel Garrard will be forwarded under separate cover.

2. Max von Linder to Brigadier Messiter
August 29th, 1936

. . . The enclosed letter fell from Colonel Garrard's wallet. There are many questions I should like to ask, but

knowing you as I do, I fear you would not answer them.
Just one, therefore: How did you discover where the
Colonel and I were sitting?

3. Brigadier Messiter to Max von Linder
August 31st, 1936

. . . I still like to keep a close eye on my people,
Max.

4. Article in Völkischer Beobachter
September 6th, 1936 (translation)

An Intimate Moment at the Games

The most illustrious page in the long history of the
Olympic Games has been written in imperishable letters.
The Captains and the Kings, the Princes and the Presi-
dents have departed, each carrying with him memories of
the Führer's courtesy as a host, his wisdom as a politician,
his devotion to the cause of peace as a world statesman. It
is now our pleasure to reveal a more intimate but equally
typical side of his character. It seems that a group of
veteran British soldiers met by chance at the stadium
before the opening ceremony. So great was their delight at
seeing one another again after an interval of almost twenty
years that their enthusiasm quite overcame their celebrated national reserve. Two, in fact, were so excited
when they caught sight of a third that they inadvertently
knocked him to the ground with their embraces as the
Führer was passing only a few feet away on his path to
light the Sacred Flame. Security guards were immediately on the alert, perhaps fearing some unseemly interruption to the dignity of the occasion, but the Führer bade
them stand back and insisted on shaking hands with two of
those concerned. "They were fighting soldiers as I was,"
he is reported as saying, "and they did their duty with
honor. It is now my duty and my honor to welcome them
to our country."

Before proceeding, he expressed the hope that their
friend, still dazed by his companions' exuberance, would

recover in time to enjoy the opening ceremonies. A small incident, perhaps, but one we feel well worth recording as typifying the Führer's spirit of comradeship toward the man in the street as well as to the great of all nations. Heil Hitler!

5. Brigadier Messiter to Colonel Garrard
December 17th, 1936

I am most relieved to learn that god-in-Harley-Street, the eminent Dr. Selfridge, has awarded you a clean bill of health. Equally, in view of the size of his own bill, that I had the foresight to arrange for it to be paid by the department. (The Holy Romans, as Anthony Charles constantly reminds me, have a point. The confessional box provides a direct line and is cheaper.)

I enclose, hopefully for your amusement, three brief memoranda of August last, relating to what may now be termed, for lack of a better title, The Incident. My intuition on that occasion was at fault. I gave you, albeit guardedly, what Harvey James would probably describe as a bum steer. However, wiser counsels re Herr Schickel-gruber prevailed in time for me to correct it via the good offices of your friends Meadows and Barnes.

I hand over the reins in a fortnight. Pray continue to serve your new masters with the loyalty and integrity with which you have always favored the old. In the meanwhile it would give us considerable pleasure if you and your dear wife would come to dinner on December 31st. Perhaps your son would accompany you. I understand he is about to enter Sandhurst, poor fellow. We shall toast the New Year together with his future. Anthony will doubtless enjoy emphasizing to him the many advantages of the horse over the tank . . .

6. General Garrard to General Messiter
June 9th, 1944

. . . Thank you for your note. I too am proud that my son took part in the D-day landings.

At the risk of repetition I am still most concerned by our continued lack of interest in and support for those brave elements in Germany who are now prepared to risk everything in order to overthrow Hitler. Can you bring some influence to bear in high places?

7. General Messiter to General Garrard
June 11th, 1944

The answer to your question is in the negative. Also, at the risk of repetition, I would remind you that I am no longer head of the department but merely a tired old warhorse, bribed (quite unnecessarily) with tardy promotion to help out for the duration. In any event, my information, limited as it is, would indicate that present policy does not favor an assassination attempt at this time. If successful, it would simply transform the bloody man into a heroic martyr. Precisely the same danger in fact which existed in August, 1936. He was riding high then and he's riding high now—or so his brainwashed followers believe. No, Adrian, he must fall and be seen to fall. A murdering maniac brought to justice, not an unvanquished votary with a voice in Valhalla. Be patient. The future brightens . . .

8. General Garrard to General Messiter
June 15th, 1944

I appreciate your alliteration, but not your optimism. No one can foresee the future. Had I done so in January, 1919, how many lives would have been spared? You once told me that all of us who had recognized the poisonous plant and not destroyed it were equally to blame. That is not true. It had not yet grown tall in Stroombeek, was not yet riding high. But I recognized it for what it was and might become, and that was my God-given chance to cut it down, but I did not take it. The fault is mine, mine alone. How many more must die because of it?

* * *

Messiter never answered my question. How could he? He was a man given to accuracy, precision. No one can ever answer it with certainty. The dead are too scattered, their numbers too vast for any man-made inventory to encompass. Only God can know the final reckoning. He and, perhaps, the Devil.

Judica me Deus. The Priest had spoken that prayer in the presence of evil, and for the rest of my life I have repeated it. *Judge me, God.* A hard prayer, surely meriting an answer of greater hardness.

Max Von Linder was hanged in July, 1944, for his part in the brave but abortive plot against the life of Hitler.

My dear son, George, was killed in action the following month and on the same day my beloved wife, Katherine, died during an enemy rocket attack on London. One friend. Two whom I loved. Three among the countless millions. And now Christine, the mother of my grandson, has gone too.

I have taken the boy to live with me in my house, but young children cannot, should not, be expected to share the weight of burdens such as mine. Perhaps one day when he is older, I shall be able to explain my prayer to him. *Judge me, but hear my plea for absolution.*

And perhaps he will understand. *Mea culpa, mea culpa, mea maxima culpa.* And, perhaps, forgive.

PART 3

THE
BLIND
MAN'S
TALE

CHAPTER 19

GOLGOTHA. January, 1919.
Writer urgently requires information.
Please contact Adrian Garrard . . .

I'd booked the advertisement to run for four consecutive days. Someone who could verify the truth or otherwise of my grandfather's narrative must still be alive. Selfridge perhaps, Meadows. I had to speak to them, had to know for sure. For a week I hardly left the flat in case one of them should call. Neither did. And then, when I'd almost given up hope, there was a message waiting on the answering machine after I'd returned from lunching with my agent. The voice was firm, surprisingly youthful.

"Henry Messiter speaking. I take it your grandfather has committed his memoirs to paper. Perhaps you would care to join me for dinner? Beaconsfield, if you can manage that. Shall we say a fortnight from today? That will afford me time to read whatever there may be if you would kindly forward it without delay. Eight P.M. suit you? Don't trouble with black tie. Quite informal."

He added his address and I wrote it down while trying to work out how old he must be. He'd officially retired at fifty-five in 1936. That was forty years ago. I checked the date he had proposed for our meeting. November 11th. Ninety-five years of age but ironic humor apparently still intact.

When I arrived, he was seated in a well-cushioned high-backed armchair watching the television news. Long columns of men marched past the Cenotaph, their poppies of remembrance pinned to their lapels, a few, the commentator explained in hushed tones, veterans of 1914–18, the War to End Wars, fewer now with every passing winter. Flames reflected from a log fire licked up around the figures on the screen.

"I only use this machine on rare occasions," Henry Messiter said. "I prefer the one in my bedroom. Far more efficacious and considerably less harmful than sleeping pills. Do sit down."

He looked, I thought, like a cross between an elderly Pickwick and a retired Mr. Chips. But behind the outward show of benevolence there was still vigilance, caution, a man long accustomed to guarding secrets.

"You didn't watch the ceremony this morning, sir—live?"

He frowned and at once I regretted my tactlessness.

At his age he probably slept till noon.

"I would hardly choose the word live to describe such an occasion," he said, "but I did indeed watch it. So many poppies for so many deaths."

He paused and his dry lips traced the faint ghost of a smile. "I watched it from the window in what was formerly known as the War Office. They still insist on sending a car each year to take me there and back. Touching. I only accept because it amuses me to think how they can possibly justify the expense." He pointed at the sideboard.

"Open that bottle of champagne would you? My thumbs have lost their former agility but my taste buds, thank God, remain intact. Your grandfather enjoyed this brand. Bollinger."

I poured glasses for us both.

"Five years more and Her Gracious Majesty will send me a birthday telegram. You will then have to treat me with the veneration and respect due to all genuine antiques. The last of those concerned with Golgotha, now your grandfather's been gathered." He touched the manuscript which lay on a small table beside his chair.

"A photocopy. I assume you have retained the original?"

I'd hoped he wouldn't notice that, but there was no point in denying it now.

"I was afraid it might get lost in the post."

"Rubbish, dear boy. You were afraid I might destroy it. Quite right. A matter of simple intelligence. Not that intelligence is ever simple."

The news ended with pictures of the French president and the German chancellor at Verdun, heads bowed, hands linked, like figures in a child's paper cutout, like the Priest and the Shouter, friends now, men of peace.

"The name of the enemy changes," Messiter said, "but not the need for one. How else would our national economies continue to flourish?"

A round-table discussion had begun on the screen.

"There are no circumstances," a young bishop was saying, "none whatsoever which can justify the taking of a human life . . ."

He dwindled to a dot in midsentence, disappeared.

Messiter chuckled. "I do so enjoy doing that. Gives one a real sense of power."

He put down the remote control switch, rang a small silver handbell. His manservant wheeled a laden dinner trolley between us, eased his master forward in the chair, added an extra cushion at his back. I realized he could no longer stand without assistance.

"Montrachet to accompany the smoked salmon," he said.

He began to eat slowly, savoring each mouthful, watching me as he did so.

"One's pleasures grow fewer with age but one's appreciation of them grows in proportion. Like one's patience." He smiled. "A quality you appear already to have cultivated."

"Is it true about Polzl?" I asked. "About Hitler?"

He peered at my empty plate.

"Do have some more smoked salmon. It doesn't keep. Dries. Curls at the edges. Such a pity."

After the meal, he handed me back the photocopy.

"May I inquire what you plan to do with this?"

"I came here in the hope that you'd advise me."

He poured himself a second glass of brandy.

"My dear friend Anthony Charles used to say that good advice is almost invariably ignored. He was correct, and for that reason I've spent a great part of my life avoiding answers to awkward questions from those in authority."

"I'm not anyone in authority."

He cupped his glass, trying to warm it. His mottled hands looked cold in spite of the fire.

"No," he said, "just another Adrian Garrard. Another earnest seeker after truth. Tiresome, but I suppose praiseworthy. How is the redoubtable Miss Wilkins? I remember suffering one of her fish pies."

"I enjoyed them," I said.

He sighed. "Like your grandfather, a glutton for punishment. He wanted to take part in a second Golgotha operation, you know. On the Somme. Near Ginchy."

"He doesn't mention that."

"Presumably because I told him he was in no fit state to do so. That annoyed him. But my judgment was sound, wouldn't you say?"

He smiled faintly.

"More often than not I dare claim that it has been. Possibly this is largely the result, as in the case of Sir Winston Churchill, of my mixed parentage. My English father taught me certain values, my American mother never to betray them. I have been entrusted with many secrets but not being wholly British like, shall we say, Messrs. Philby, Burgess or Maclean, I have kept them to myself."

The unusually long speech, the bitter little joke at the end, seemed to have tired him. It was some time before he was able to lean forward and tap the manuscript.

"Do what you will with this, my boy, but grant me one favor. Wait until I'm dead before you do it. It shouldn't be too long."

"Is it all true, sir? I must know. Please tell me."

He took off his spectacles and as he wiped moisture from them I was able to see his eyes for the first time. They were veiled, clouded and dim, like those of an old dog, immensely weary.

"I thought I already had," he said quietly. "Otherwise, why should I have asked you to wait?" He replaced his spectacles.

"Now if you'll forgive me, I'm a little tired. The soporific television upstairs beckons. Perhaps that youthful bishop will still be spouting his nonsense."

"Is it nonsense?"

He drained the last drops of his brandy.

"Immaculate theology, were it not for the undoubted existence of evil—of devils."

He thrust himself forward in his chair and the firelight flashed in the thick lenses, twin points of fury. His voice was suddenly strong and sure with an anger undimmed by time.

"I wish to God your grandfather had shot the bloody man at Stroombeek in 1919. I wish to God I'd let him do it seventeen years later in Berlin."

His whole body sagged as though the effort had drained all its remaining strength. I caught him by the shoulders, eased him back against the cushions, felt the pathetically protruding bones, the utter frailty of his being. His next words were no more than a faint whisper, and although he used my name, he was no longer speaking to me.

"So much suffering could have been avoided, Adrian. So many lives spared. But the guilt is not yours. It belongs to all of us. I told you that. All who knew."

After a few seconds his head lifted suddenly, the hidden eyes staring into mine.

"Let us remember," he said, "but let us also pray. Never again." He leaned toward me, a final effort. "You will wait, won't you?"

"I'll wait," I said.

He missed the royal telegram by six months and I missed his memorial service because I had to go to Paris that January to meet a television producer who wanted someone to write a series about two American teenagers who had signed on as crew for a yacht in the Mediterranean and found themselves involved in drug smuggling. Modern stuff. Up-to-date. After that, I thought, I'll go to Ypres, the salient, Stroombeek. I'd no idea of what I'd do when I got there, only that I had to see it. I cashed in the producer's return air ticket, took the car by ferry to Calais instead. I'd need it for the trip to Flanders later, but that wasn't the only reason. I disliked the idea of leaving the Colt revolver behind in my flat for someone to steal and hold up pensioners outside post offices, equally that of having it detected by one of the X-ray machines at Heathrow. So I hid it in my suitcase and drove to Paris.

The producer explained that his project was in its infancy and wide open to ideas. He spent two hours listening to mine and, when his secretary had got them all down in shorthand, remembered he had a lunch date and said we'd keep in touch. I never saw him again, and, so far, have not seen his series either. But the

residue of profit on his air ticket would take care of all expenses to
Ypres and home again. That, as they say, is show business.

I took the autoroute north out of Paris, the names of places on
either side streaming past like those of half-forgotten battle honors
on old and tattered flags. Compiègne, St.-Quentin, Peronne,
Bapaume, Arras. For a good part of the way I realized I was
traveling along the approximate line of what had once been the
western front. I stopped at Compiègne, visited the Glade of the
Armistice, the replica of the railway carriage where the peace of
victory had been signed in 1918, that of defeat in 1940. In an inner
hall, viewing machines were ranged on either side of the Flame of
Remembrance. By turning their handles one could see stereoscopic
photographs of the trenches, the mud, blood, and horror of the
First World War. There were none of the Second. I remember one
in particular. A young French boy peering with amusement at a
very correct-looking German officer, one of their Armistice delegation, perhaps aping his military bearing. The boy looks happy. He
knows the war is over. He would, I reckoned, have been nearly
thirty when it began again in 1939.

I stayed the night in Arras and the following morning found the
French headquarters of the Commonwealth War Graves Commission at Beauraine, told them I was on my way to Ypres. They were
very helpful, recommended a visit to the Museum of the Salient in
the Cloth Hall, gave me one of their maps of war cemeteries and
memorials, each one marked with a numbered colored circle. By
far the biggest cluster was around Ypres. There must have been a
hundred at least, sprouting out around the town like the petals of
some enormous overblown white and purple flower, blooms of
death.

I was there by noon. A man sweeping the pavement outside
the Cloth Hall told me the museum was closed, wouldn't reopen
until the tourist season began again in the spring.

"But we still sound the Last Post at the Menin Gate," he said,
"every day at sundown. Nine o'clock in the summer, six in the
winter."

"We?"

He smiled. "It used to be soldiers from the British Royal
Artillery, but now it's done by two members of our city fire
brigade."

I thanked him and said something about supposing our army was a bit short-handed these days.

"They still use silver bugles," he said. "You should not miss it."

I drove out of the town, found myself on the Messines road. The famous ridge didn't look in the least threatening, no more than a gentle undulation in the flat countryside. I tried to imagine it covered with big guns. On a street corner a Belgian teenager was strumming a guitar, singing a rock number to a group of other kids. He was obviously doing his best to appear suitably angry and threatening, but just couldn't manage it. In my limited experience the Belgians are a naturally gentle, rather docile, people. Until they get behind the wheel of a car. Then they become fiends. I asked a boy with a Union Jack sewn onto his rucksack which direction I should take to find the road to Passchendaele.

"Passchendaele," he said. "Never heard of it, mate."

I went back into Ypres, discovered a sign marked St.-Julien. A grey-white mist hung like a pall over the road, the sky was leaden. I felt an overwhelming sense of foreboding, oppression. It wasn't only the weather, not just the forest of green signs pointing to the military burial places. The whole area seemed impregnated with an atmosphere of sadness, despair. I was in the salient on the road to Passchendaele barely five miles away. The cemeteries had very ordinary names, homely. Buffs Road, Cement House, Minty Farm. I stopped before Passchendaele at the largest one, Tyne Cot. Rows and rows of neat identical headstones, thousands upon thousands, many inscribed simply A Soldier of the Great War. Known unto God. I passed by them, wondering. Sergeant Wilkins, perhaps, father of Hilda? There was no sound but the wind. Major Richardson? Soon, I thought, it must rain and I remembered how he had described it. "God's tears." Well, the divine weeping had lasted now for more than sixty years and showed no signs of ceasing. I walked out of the big gates and saw a wooden blue and white printed sign planted at the roadside pointing to the right: "Route '14–'18." So men remembered too. Here at least. And not just for two minutes each year. In their stark simplicity, that sign and the others like it were more moving than any granite cenotaph. I followed them up the hill to Passchendaele.

There was mud round the battlefield memorial which stands at the crest of the ridge, guarding and dominating the town which the Canadians it commemorates had finally taken. The rain had begun.

A group of winter tourists were huddled in mackintoshes near the obelisk. Americans, English, French, Germans, as well as Canadians. Their bus waited at the roadside while its driver addressed them in a mixture of languages, pointing out the various landmarks. I asked him if he could tell me the whereabouts of the Stroombeek Valley, but apart from a frown of irritation at the interruption, he ignored the question, continued with his set piece.

"It lies there," a tall man said in English and pointed down the hill. He must have been well into his seventies but he wore no coat, simply a high-necked sweater. He seemed oblivious of the rain. I looked in the direction he'd indicated. Green pastureland, a few plowed fields, a thicket of trees, a couple of small farmhouses.

"You're sure?" I asked him.

"Quite sure," he said and smiled. "Those trees. They're in the middle of it."

I thanked him, stared at the unremarkable view for another minute, then turned and walked back to the car, conscious of anticlimax.

I lost my way in the rain, finally arrived back at Ypres by way of the Menin road, saw a line of stationary cars ahead of me outside the Memorial Gate. It was one minute to six. I pulled into a parking place, ran toward the arch, arrived just in time to see two young men in duffel coats and jeans sounding the Last Post beneath it. It echoed and reechoed under the great curved stone ceiling. When they'd finished, they tucked their silver bugles under their arms and walked away chatting to each other. From either direction traffic began to flow again. I moved forward, stood on the pavement under the center of the arch, looked up at the apparently endless roll of names carved into its walls.

"Fifty-five thousand of them," a voice said beside me, "all with no known grave."

I turned and saw the tall elderly Englishman from Passchendaele standing beside me. He still didn't have a coat, just the sweater.

"What were they wearing?" he asked.

"Sorry?"

"The buglers. What sort of clothes?"

I told him.

"That's right," he said, "that's how it should be. They're sick of uniforms, they are."

For the second time I wondered what on earth he was talking about.

"Who?" I asked.

His fingers touched the nearest names on the wall, very gently, almost a caress.

"This lot. I come to see them the first Sunday every year. Just to say hullo and sorry."

I stared at him.

"But you didn't see the buglers?"

"I'm blind," he said.

I felt a surge of excitement. It couldn't be possible. It would have been too much of a coincidence.

"You showed me the Stroombeek valley," I said.

"Oh, it's you, is it? Thought I recognized the voice. That's right. I showed you the Stroombeek."

"But . . ."

"You don't have to see a place to know it's there," he said. "Same with men." He touched the names again, another row. "You don't have to see them to know they're here," he said.

"Were you in that war? In the salient?"

He smiled, his blind eyes looking at the wall.

"Don't like guns," he said. "Never did."

I had to know, had somehow to ask him.

"My name's Garrard," I said. "Adrian Garrard."

I was watching his face very closely, but his expression didn't alter, contained no flicker of recognition.

"If I had my way," he said, "I'd throw away all the guns. Every last one of them."

I continued to watch him as he moved through the arch, one hand trailing along the inscribed wall, guiding his path. Then I hurried to catch up, help him.

"It's all right," he said. "I stay at the same pension just round the corner each time. I'm used to finding my way in the darkness. Had a long training. Good-night then, Mr. Garrard."

I wanted to follow him, to ask him more, but decided against it. If I was right, he wouldn't tell me. If I wasn't, it wouldn't matter anyway. I walked slowly back to the car, turned it round. He hadn't told me what I wanted to know, but he had told me something else. I knew now what I must do before I left that place.

An hour later I was on the road to the nearest cross-channel port.

CHAPTER 20

Dunkirk is not principally renowned for the quality of its hotels, but it was too late to catch a boat that day so I found the one Michelin considered the most comfortable, went to the reception desk, booked a room for the night. Even without the sound of her voice behind me, I'd have recognized her. The smell of the rich perfume was unmistakable.

"Adrian, darling. Where the hell have you *been* all my life?"

I turned and Boss Lady gathered me to her mink-covered bosom. She was back in films, she told me, an independent producer and *loaded*. The oil business, money excepted, was just a lot of balls. What was I doing that I shouldn't be?

We had dinner in her suite, the only one in the hotel. She was in this Godforsaken place conducting a quick location reconnaissance. Tomorrow she would be in Brussels, en route for the battlefield of Waterloo. There were, thank the same God, decent hotels in Brussels. She had ordered a bottle of Remy Martin.

"To old times," she said, raising her glass. "We none of us live forever."

I smiled at her, considered the invitation. My bedroom was small, ugly, unwelcoming. Hers was the opposite in every respect. None of us did live forever and she was still very beautiful. "So's an A-bomb till it explodes," Spencer had warned.

I decided to ignore him.

"Old times," I said and we clinked glasses across the table. The explosion, such as it was, came much later.

"This time," she said, lying naked in the huge bed beside me, "this time nothing's going to stop me doing what I want."

I knew only too well what was coming next.

"Remember that great concept I always had? The hinges of history. Okay. Well, forget the Roman Empire, all that balls. Take a couple of for instances. Suppose the British *hadn't* got their guys off these beaches here at Dunkirk? Suppose what's his name, Blücher, *hadn't* showed in the nick of time at Waterloo? Suppose someone you've never heard of makes some decision or maybe doesn't make it, I don't know, and the whole goddam world sort of changes course as a result?"

Her voice was impatient, eager, full of enthusiasm.

"After Brussels, I go straight to London, find myself a writer. Unless you can come up with something. You got any ideas, Adrian?"

I stared at the ceiling and thought of what my grandfather had written. The crawling creatures in the mud before Passchendaele, the men who'd perished there and the others who'd perished beneath it, the Priest, the Shouter, the bundles of rags, Askew. I imagined the smell of the gas, the face of Polzl, and remembered the French boy in the photograph at Compiègne, grinning his welcome to peace, the boy who'd have grown up after the war to end wars, in good time to be destroyed by the next, its sequel, its continuation made inevitable by one man, Adolf Hitler. I thought of my father and Katherine and Max von Linder and the millions who'd died and might have lived if the other Adrian Garrard had been able to pull the trigger that day in Golgotha. And I felt the searing magnitude of his guilt as though, like his name, it were my own.

That's when the explosion came.

"Jesus! I asked you a question five minutes ago. You never used to be slow with answers. What the hell's happened to you, for Christ's sake?"

"I was just thinking," I said.

"Oh balls. Forget it. I need my beauty sleep. Good-*night*. Good-*bye*."

She turned away, reached for her eye mask, put it on, shutting out the world.

I returned to my unwelcoming room and, in the morning, caught the first ferry for England.

I'd hoped that the blind man might be on board, but he wasn't. Perhaps he'd stayed to pay one more visit to Stroombeek as I had done the evening before. If he was the Acolyte, he'd have had good reason.

"You don't have to see them to know they're here."

He had given me mine, too.

"Throw away the guns. Every last one of them."

It had still been raining as I walked down into the deserted valley, slipping and slithering in the darkness on the soggy grass. With a torch I'd found the small thicket of trees, felt my way into it between the dripping trunks, the trailing branches. I'd half expected to discover bits of rusting metal, pieces of rag, perhaps even a skull. There was nothing, except for two shallow indentations in the damp grass, each about twenty feet wide. I'd slid down into the first of them, knelt on the earth, dug a hole with a screwdriver I'd brought from the car. When it was deep enough, I'd dropped the Colt revolver into it, covered it with the displaced soil, stamped it down firmly until the gun was completely hidden. If anyone ever found it, they'd surely leave it there, another useless relic, another ugly reminder of the bitter harvest spawned on Route '14-'18.

The rain had stopped by the time I left the thicket, and the dark racing clouds had cleared the moon. Its pale silvery light shone down on the valley.

I heard singing. A man's voice. My heart seemed to stop beating as I looked back at the trees. Then I realized the sound wasn't coming from there but from one of the farmhouses beyond. There was music too. The words were in French but I recognized the tune. The Twenty-third Psalm. The Shouter had sung it here in German for the Priest and for the soul of his friend Shaw.

"Though I walk through the valley of the shadow of death I shall fear no evil . . ."

He'd sung it here in this same month of January.

The first Sunday in every year. Just to say hullo and sorry.

I turned away, walked quickly from the place of Golgotha.